BETWEEN WORLDS 6

MISSING HOME

LORI WOLF-HEFFNER

HEAD IN THE GROUND PUBLISHING

ISBN (Paperback Edition) 978-1-989465-12-7

ISBN (Ebook Edition) 978-1-989465-13-4

ISBN (Large Print Edition) 978-1-989465-14-1

Some characters and events in this book are fictitious. Any similarity to real persons, living or dead, is coincidental and not intended by the author.

Editing by Susan Fish

Cover design by Fresh Design

All photographs from Shutterstock

Head in the Ground Publishing

Waterloo, Ontario, Canada

headintheground.com

✺ Created with Vellum

Dedicated to Elisabeta Wolf (1836-1914), a woman who suffered many losses and yet was still the rock of her family.

CHAPTER ONE

"So you saw a counsellor, then?"

Juliana held her phone to her ear. "Yeah. It was good. Don't get me wrong—this is really depressing and I'm still scared but I think we understand everything at least a bit better now."

"That's good," Jasmine said. "My dad says a lot of times people don't take time to talk things out. It's really good all four of you went."

Juliana had seen the therapist with her mom, her Aunt Anne, and her cousin Sophie after Opa—Juliana's grandfather—had started hallucinating that he was back in his childhood home in Eastern Europe and that his mother was still alive, even though she had died a long time ago.

"The weirdest part, though," Juliana said, "was that he thought both Sophie and I were his mom. It didn't matter who spoke, me or Sophie. And then he started talking to his mother as though she were sick. It seriously looked like he wanted one of us to lay on top of the television." She fought back a giggle. "Oh, man. I really shouldn't laugh about that. It wasn't funny when it happened."

"I get it. My parents have developed a pretty dark sense of humour—comes with the stresses of being a nurse and a police officer. Trust me—I'm speaking from experience here—you need to be a little understanding with yourself. You've been through a lot."

As much as Juliana appreciated Jasmine's attempts at comforting her, she still felt guilty for even thinking it was funny. Opa was losing his memories to Alzheimer's. There was nothing funny about that. The stress of moving from Calgary to Kitchener a few months before hardly compared with saving people's lives every day. Stressful, yes, but Juliana would rather have to move cities than have a job where the wrong decision could cause someone to die. She shivered at the thought and then came back to the topic at hand.

"But why does he always think he's back in Semlak, his village in Romania? So far as I know he's lived in Canada for at least forty years, maybe even longer. That's more than half his life."

"Mom says that dementia patients often regress to their childhoods."

Juliana didn't doubt Jasmine—her mom worked as an

ER nurse—but it just didn't make sense to her. "But why? There are a lot of things about my childhood I'd rather forget."

"Also lots you're happy to remember. I bet you'd be glad to remember all the sleepovers you had with friends like Rachel."

Jasmine was right. Rachel had been Juliana's best friend in Calgary. Even though Juliana hadn't been able to be there for Rachel when her mom died this winter and even though they only talked once a week or so now, Juliana still considered Rachel a part of her family. She missed her.

"But some of it probably has to do with the simple fact that he grew up in Romania," Jasmine said. "All my grand-parents talked about home—Guatemala and Yugoslavia— and about how wonderful it was, despite the wars they lived through."

"Yugoslavia...? Oh. That's what the country was called before it split, right?" Juliana didn't pay much attention to what happened in the rest of the world. She hadn't even known a country called Yugoslavia had ever existed in Europe until Jasmine had told her about it.

"Yeah. Dad was born in Serbia, but he still says that Yugoslavia is his home. I don't know. I was born here, so I have no idea about any of that."

"I wonder what I'll think about when I'm older," Juliana said. "I spent my whole childhood in Calgary. I had lots of good friends, but I only saw my mom's family over Skype. I saw my grandfather..." Juliana paused as she tried to count. "No idea, but not a lot. I mean, I said hi on the phone at Christmas and Easter, and then the odd Skype call with Aunt Anne's family, but that was pretty much it."

"I wouldn't worry about it too much," Jasmine said. "By the time we're that old, they'll have a cure for Alzheimer's. In the meantime, I'd better get off the phone. I have to practise. One of the judges at the last competition said I shouldn't take so long to plié before I jump. I'll get higher if I can fix that."

Juliana envied Jasmine's dance ability. She was the best in their age group at the studio and had taken home a scholarship for top dancer in their age group for jazz at the last competition. As the worst on their team, Juliana still needed to improve a lot. But she had worked really hard over March Break. Her teacher, Miss Denise, had told Juliana that she had improved considerably since first starting at Kitchener Dance Academy. *At least my dancing is getting better*, she thought. *My marks at school are a different story.*

"I'm going to work on my pirouettes," Juliana said. "Thanks to your tips, I've almost got my triple."

"Sounds good. I'll see you at practice tonight."

After the girls hung up, Juliana thought about Calgary and how much she missed it. A few weeks before, in geography class, she had had to write about what gave her a sense of place in Kitchener. It was hard to write, because at that time she'd only been in Kitchener about a month. She was beginning to adjust to the move. Finally. But Calgary was still home to her. Jasmine was right.

"Semlak was your home too, wasn't it?" Juliana addressed the brown, leather-bound book of drawings on the night table where she placed her phone. Shortly after her arrival in Kitchener, Juliana had found this book, her great-grandmother's sketchbook, in Opa's basement. Opa had said his mother, who Juliana called Omama, had completed the drawings when she was Juliana's age and lived in Semlak. Opa could easily explain some drawings but not all of them. They were like puzzles or mysteries to Juliana. Why had Omama drawn a lantern on one page, for example? Even though Juliana didn't understand what the drawings were about, she still loved them. She had discovered that lantern drawing one night when her anger was so intense it was burning to get out; the drawing had so much life in it and it reflected what Juliana had been feeling in a way words couldn't express.

Juliana understood she would never meet her great-grandmother but the more she learned about her drawings, the closer Omama's distant life came to Juliana's own. "You're kind of like my imaginary friend," Juliana said out loud, smiling to herself. "Only you were real and this is the proof." Juliana hugged the book to her chest. "Thank you," she whispered.

"Yulika!"

The nickname "Yulika" told Juliana who was calling her: Opa. Sometimes he called her Yuliana. With his German accent, he never seemed to start her name with a J sound.

"Yeah?" She placed the book in the drawer in her night table and opened her bedroom door.

"I'm going to shovel! Do you want to join me?"

Juliana didn't like shovelling snow, but with both parents at work—Mom managed a grocery store and Dad drove a truck, often long-haul—Opa would need the help. Aunt Anne and Uncle Phillip's family had helped Opa with chores, but they had six kids and a full schedule and couldn't always keep an eye on him, even though they lived only a three-minute walk away. When Opa began to need more care, Juliana's family, the Roths, had moved halfway across the country in order to be there for him. *Which meant shovelling*, Juliana thought with a sigh. *But he might tell me more stories about Omama.*

"Sure!" she said. She grabbed her jacket, hat, mitts, and scarf from the hallway closet and bundled up. She stepped outside and Opa handed her a shovel.

Juliana pushed the shovel across the driveway, bent her knees, hoisted its load over the snowbank, and walked back to the other side. Rinse and repeat. Thankfully, Opa's driveway was only a single-width driveway. Unfortunately, it was two cars long.

Opa used a much smaller shovel to scoop up a little

snow and throw it to the side of the driveway instead of over the snowbank. Juliana would have to lift that snow over the snowbank herself later, but the counsellor had said that Opa needed exercise and that it was best to avoid pointing out his mistakes.

"The further along his dementia progresses," the counsellor had said, "the more he's going to feel like everyone's criticizing him. So, if it's not important, it's best to just let things be."

"I can't wait to go to your competition with you," Opa said, taking a break to lean on his shovel.

"Me neither," Juliana said over the scratching of her shovel on the driveway. "Miss Denise—that's one of my dance teachers—said I really improved this week. She didn't have to stop any of my dances because I'd made a mistake."

Opa looked confused.

"That's a good thing," Juliana said, and Opa smiled and nodded. "It means I know my dances really well now and won't mess up onstage." After a pause she added, "Well, at least I hope not." Juliana had only begun to learn these competition dances during Christmas break, whereas the rest of the studio had started back in September. Juliana normally competed in solos and duets, too, but Mom and Miss Denise had decided that four groups this year would be enough for her.

Opa jabbed his shovel at a piece of ice to split it but he

gave up after the second attempt. "I remember when Katy once got a sixty-five. I think she was maybe fourteen. Same age as you! She was crying. The judge was nice to her. But he said it's important for everyone to hear what he thought because that's how everyone learns."

Juliana's eyes almost popped out of her head. "Mom got a sixty-five? And the judge gave her his comments in front of *everyone*?"

"Of course! They always did that." He pointed a gloved finger at Juliana, "Let me tell you, Yulika, she practised a lot harder after that. That is where you get it from."

Juliana couldn't remember anyone ever getting a mark in the sixties. *You'd have to be comatose to get that low*, she thought. How horrible had Mom danced that day? Juliana continued shovelling while Opa kept talking.

"That was when your mom wouldn't listen to anything I or your *oma* said. If we asked her to clean her side of the room, she wouldn't touch it. If we asked her to leave it messy, she'd clean it. I wanted to tell her about her grandmother—Omama—she was such a wonderful person." He shook his head. "But Katy wouldn't listen. Peter always listened and Annie, well, she sometimes did and sometimes didn't. But by the time Katy was your age...I don't know what happened."

"She always wants me to listen," Juliana replied.

Opa laughed and picked up his shovel again. "She's a mother now and understands. Do you have any friends?"

Opa's abrupt changes in conversation no longer surprised Juliana. Sometimes they annoyed her, like when she wanted to ask more about his mother and he suddenly remembered something completely different he wanted to take care of. But sometimes, like right now, she welcomed the shift. The conversation was getting awkward with him talking about her mom. Besides, how would Juliana know what Mom had been thinking back then? *I wasn't even alive!* she thought.

"Well, there's Meghan and Shawna at school. And you've met Jasmine," she said.

Opa stopped shovelling as he tried to remember. "The one on your computer?"

Juliana laughed. "No, that was Rachel."

"The one whose mother was killed in a car accident."

Juliana sighed. "Yes."

"Your friend from home."

Juliana nodded. "I miss her."

"And you're not best friends with her anymore, right?"

Was this what Opa remembered? All the bad things that had happened recently? What happened to all his good memories about his home?

"Did you fight?" Opa asked.

"No!" Juliana shouted, making Opa jump. "I'm sorry," she said, immediately regretting her outburst. Rachel's mom had been killed by a drunk driver last month. Some of the wounds from that time were still fresh.

"I said something wrong again, didn't I?" Opa said.

Juliana shook her head. "It's nothing."

"Now, Yuliana—" but before Opa could say anything more, a taxi pulled up to the end of the driveway.

"Dad!" Juliana cried, throwing her shovel to the side and running to the car. Because the Roths only had one car and Dad was often gone for days on end with his truck, he took a cab to and from his work.

Dad paid the driver and stepped out of the car, dragging a sports bag behind him. Juliana wrapped her arms around him.

"Hey," Dad said. "It's nice to see you, too." To Opa he said, "Hi, Peter."

Opa waved back and threw a small amount of snow to the side of the driveway.

Dad whispered into Juliana's ear, "Why is he doing that?"

"He wanted to shovel. The counsellor said we shouldn't criticize him unless it's really important."

Dad nodded. "Peter, why don't you hand me that and go back inside. The snow looks pretty heavy."

Opa gave Dad the shovel without question. "You two don't see each other enough," he said. "Family is important." He headed back into the house.

Dad looked quizzically at Juliana. "Were the two of you just talking about me?"

"No—he might be having another blip."

'Blip' was what Mom called Opa's intermittent brain problems. The term fit.

"Let me take my bag inside and make sure he's okay. Then I'll tackle that rocky mess at the end of the driveway—the cab almost couldn't get over it."

Dad was in and out of the house in three minutes. "He's watching CNN," he reported. Opa loved his news—the local newspaper came every morning, he made sure he turned the television on for the local six o'clock news, and whenever he was bored, he turned on a news station on television or the radio.

As Dad tackled the frozen snow and ice the snow-plough had shoved onto the end of the driveway, Juliana told him about school.

"Shawna suggested I join the dance club. I thought it'd be a cool idea. Can I?"

"This semester has been hard on you," Dad said. "Are you sure you want to take on more commitments?"

"I'm sure I can handle it. Besides, Shawna said I can use the shows we do for my community service hours. I talked to the teacher in charge already—it's actually Ms. Lee, my English teacher—and she said yes."

Dad heaved a boulder of frozen slush to the side. "I'd forgotten about those hours."

In Ontario, all high school students had to complete forty hours of community service before graduating from high school.

"I get my homework done every day. And joining the dance club will make practising more interesting. It's kind of boring rehearsing the same four dances all the time. And if I don't get better at my dancing, I won't make it into the apprenticeship program next year."

If Juliana had stayed in Calgary, she would've already been a part of her old studio's apprenticeship program, where she would've learned how to teach. That she couldn't take part in it this year still upset her. However, now that she knew her family better, she was kind of happy that they had moved, even if meant waiting a year before apprenticing. *But next year I want to be in that program*, she thought.

"I don't know," Dad said as he rammed the shovel into some ice, splitting it into pieces. "I still think it'll be too much for you. Besides, you're already practising lots. I really think you should focus more on your schooling, especially after you got so upset about your marks last semester."

"But next year I'll be in that apprenticeship program plus my full competition schedule plus school...isn't it better to get ahead? And this'll be good practice."

"Can't you do these hours in the summer?"

"Yeah, but not with the dance club, obviously. I'd be stuck helping in some admin thing or picking up garbage or something like that."

Dad studied her for a moment.

"Please...?"

Dad heaved another pile of ice off the driveway and studied his daughter one more time. She gave him the best puppy dog eyes she could. She wasn't particularly skilled at looking convincing, but short of begging, no other ideas came to her.

Dad nodded. Juliana jumped in excitement, lost her footing on uncovered ice, and fell into the snowbank. Dad rushed over to her to check if she was okay, but by then she was already laughing. Sometimes her excitement overwhelmed her, too.

CHAPTER TWO

*E*lisabeth couldn't figure out what she felt. She was angry about her first destination, had mixed emotions about the second one, and was excited and nervous about the third. Today was Palm Sunday and Elisabeth's confirmation, the day she would become an adult in the church. But that was only if she completed all steps in the ritual and passed the public examination.

Elisabeth waited by the front gate to her home, trying to remain calm while all her emotions whirled around inside her.

"Hurry up," Mammi said to Elisabeth's younger siblings as she shooed them out of the house. "Cows walk faster than the three of you!"

Elisabeth stared in wonder at her family because Mammi had taken extra special care with everyone's clothing: crisp pleats in the girls' wide skirts and Luki's pants, strongly starched underskirts, and linen shirts and blouses so smoothly ironed that Elisabeth had to believe that God had had a hand in it. The only item that Mammi had not prepared was everyone's footwear: Luki, only eight but already learning Tata's trade, had cleaned Mammi's and the girls' satin slippers and had polished his own leather boots.

As her siblings walked through the poultry yard and the front yard toward Elisabeth, she couldn't help but think of her own clothing: she wore a white blouse with the buttons hugged by white satin ribbons sewn down the front, and a flowing embroidery pattern—also stitched in white—next to the ribbons. Her narrow sleeves puffed slightly at the shoulder and ended in lovely lace cuffs. Every pleat on her white skirt was perfectly pressed, her four underskirts starched stiff, and the dark blue apron on top was so smooth it didn't even have folds in it. Over her shoulders she wore a gorgeous, green cashmere shawl Mammi had embroidered in a colourful but delicate floral pattern. In her hand-purse, Elisabeth carried a white handkerchief Anna had embroidered for her, and on her feet she wore the black satin slippers Luki had cleaned. Rosina was still too young to contribute anything to Elisabeth's confirmation wardrobe but she had helped that morning by holding Elisabeth's white beaded hairband while Anna braided Elisabeth's hair, which was now pinned at the top of her head.

Today was an important day and Elisabeth didn't want to let anyone down. She had studied hard, but her mind was still filled with worries because there were still several steps she had to complete before the end of the ceremony, including asking her godparents and grandmother for forgiveness.

None of those three people could ever be described as friendly, kind, and loving.

Her godparents were Tata's brother and sister-in-law, Konrad-Bátschi and Margarethe-Néni. They didn't like Elisabeth's family, and everyone in Elisabeth's family—except Tata, somehow—didn't like them. How could she honestly ask them for forgiveness when she didn't feel she'd every wronged them? Furthermore, she had to promise to honour them. How could she honour such mean people?

Then there was Omama, Mammi's mother. What mood would she be in when they arrived at Mammi's family home? Omama was usually cross about something or other, and she had once even tried to convince Elisabeth to hit Luki so he would listen to her. Thankfully, God had helped Elisabeth by giving her another idea to make him obey.

After those visits would come the church ceremony. Would Elisabeth be able to answer Pastor Fröhlich's questions during the public examination with the entire congregation watching?

"Lissika," Mammi said as all five started walking to Konrad-Bátschi's house, "are you still worried about asking Konrad and Margarethe for forgiveness?"

Elisabeth nodded and silently asked Jesus for help. Not only did she hope He would calm her worries but also that He would help her honestly promise to love and honour her godparents.

"You have very little time to settle your problems with them," Mammi said.

Most Germans lived in the northern half of Semlak, and the other Schuhmacher household was on the next street to the west of Elisabeth's home so it took only a few minutes to walk there. This left Elisabeth very little time to sort out her dilemma.

Mammi continued, "If you don't recite the words that Pastor Fröhlich taught you, you cannot be confirmed." Her eyes drilled into Elisabeth's. "And you know what that means."

Elisabeth knew very well. If she did not receive her confirmation today, she would have to wait until next year to try again. That would mean another year of not being able to attend dances or being able to look for a husband, not to mention how much everyone—including her own family—would ridicule her. It also would mean being the oldest child up in the balcony of the church where all children sat. *That would be almost as bad as being the oldest woman sitting with all who are confirmed but not married*, she thought.

The unmarried adults sat at the front beside the altar, where the entire church could see which young people had still not married.

Konrad-Bátschi was Tata's older and only brother, and as such, he had inherited their father's blacksmithing workshop and most of their father's land. He was a big man who never held back his opinions, no matter how much they hurt someone else. Margarethe-Néni, Elisabeth's aunt, lived by the same rules. They disapproved of Tata's decision to travel to America to work in a factory, and they made use of every opportunity to say so.

"Find a way," Mammi said, "even if all you can do is just say the words."

Had it only been about their comments, Elisabeth would have found it easier to honour them. Everyone had opinions, whether it was gossip about Wagner Anni's crooked nose, or Pastor Fröhlich's latest sermon, where he again praised the virtues of staying with Hungary despite Semlak now belonging to Romania. But she didn't know if she could honour her godparents because of how they treated their oldest son.

"Then I'd be lying," Elisabeth said.

Their oldest son, Georg, was twenty-nine. He had fought in that great war that had almost torn apart Europe. His first wife and child had died while he was fighting, and the years he had spent on the front had left him with horrific nightmares that sometimes engulfed him during the day. Nearly everyone in the village ridiculed him, especially the Germans, but also including his own parents. Elisabeth's uncle had actually punched Georg and left him trapped in one of his nightmares in front of a crowd of onlookers. Then Elisabeth had heard Konrad-Bátschi say words she wouldn't think any father would *ever* say to his son: that he wished Georg had died in the war.

Now Mammi furrowed her brow. "Elisabeth Schuhmacher, I should hope that you would honour your godparents. They're not nice people, but they have raised their children, they support their family and church, are hard workers, and, being your godparents, if anything had ever happened to both me and your father, they would have taken you in. They understand what duty is and they carry it out every day."

Elisabeth understood all that, but she couldn't erase the picture in her mind of Georg covered in gravel, his face as white as the clouds from fear and exhaustion, realizing his father had left him while the war raged in his mind. *That's not love*, she thought, *that's hate.*

As they neared Konrad-Bátschi's house, Anna crept closer to Elisabeth. Although Anna could be a pitchfork in Elisabeth's side, Anna feared their aunt and uncle: she had once seen Georg lose himself in a fit, only to be slapped by his mother. The situation had frightened nine-year-old Anna.

"I think Georg can be nice," said Rosina, who never worried about what adults thought. Elisabeth wondered if she had acted the same way herself when she was six.

Mammi glared at her and demanded that she not say that again.

"Well, he is," Rosina insisted.

Mammi wanted to say more, but they had come up to the front gates of Konrad-Bátschi and Margarethe-Néni's house. It looked like almost every other German house in Semlak: all the walls painted in white lime, with two windows at the front, the main entrance at the side into the kitchen, and several yards along the side of the property, including the front garden for flowers, followed by the poultry yard, and then the kitchen garden at the very back. The main differ-ence between this Schuhmacher house and Elisabeth's, though, was that this one had a shingle roof. Elisabeth's home still had a thatched roof, which Tata hoped to replace with shingles once he earned enough money in America.

Before entering the property, Mammi hissed in Elisa-beth's ear, "Your heart is only open for those who act as you expect them to. But you are not a mother. At the very least have pity on them: their son did not return. Before the war, Georg was his father's pride, and he came back from the war his humiliation."

Without even asking if Elisabeth was ready, Mammi opened the gate and led her family through the front garden and poultry yard. She knocked on the side door, leaving Elisabeth only a few breaths to find a way to honestly proceed with the ritual.

Margarethe-Néni opened the door and invited the family inside. Like Mammi, she was dressed in black from her headscarf down to her shoes except for the traditional white and green stripes of her knitted socks. Konrad-Bátschi wore dark, woollen pants, a beige, linen shirt, a woollen vest, and leather house shoes. However, his cheek was bruised. Elisabeth didn't ask from what: he had either had an accident in his blacksmithing workshop, which would embarrass him to admit, or he had fought Georg during another fit.

"Elisabeth!" Eva, Georg's second wife, who was only four years older than Elisabeth, stretched out her arms as she glided toward her and embraced her. Elisabeth felt the bump protruding from Eva's belly and smiled but said nothing: she knew one didn't ask about another woman's baby. For a time, Elisabeth believed that Eva had been no different from other women: loud and gossiping. But as Elisabeth got to know her better, she saw a different side to her: Eva was at times embarrassed by and at other times concerned about her husband. Elisabeth understood that being married to Georg was not easy for her.

"Georg!" Konrad-Bátschi called out with a growl. "You have both your legs still. Use them!"

Elisabeth winced. Georg emerged from the front room, his usual cigarette perched between his fingers, his face still. He nodded, and Elisabeth smiled back. He usually said very little, and she respected that.

"It's been over a year and I still have this poor excuse for a son," Konrad-Bátschi said.

Elisabeth couldn't bear to look Georg in the eyes after such a comment. At the same time, the comment proved that Mammi was right, in a way: the war had changed not only Georg but others in the village, too. Peter-Bátschi, Mammi's brother, drank more often now. Stefan, Georg's only friend, had lost an arm and had just returned after two years in Russian captivity. And of course, two of Mammi's brothers had not returned at all, along with forty-nine other men in their Lutheran congregation. The war had not been easy on any family in Semlak, and that included her aunt and uncle. Elisabeth focused on that grain of truth as she recited what Pastor Fröhlich had taught:

"Because I have resolved to accept Holy Communion today for the very first time, I am reminded that I have sinned against God and against you and that I have sometimes deliberately and wantonly offended and angered you. Therefore, for Jesus's sake, I ask you to forgive me my missteps and sins. I promise also in the future to honour and love you, to observe the will of God and therefore to better my life. Amen."

To her surprise, Konrad-Bátschi and Margarethe-Néni nodded in response. Then Margarethe-Néni handed her a small package. Elisabeth knew her godparents would give her a little something—that was tradition. At the same time, respecting and honouring your oldest son was also tradition. Had they chosen to say something mean or to not give Elisabeth a gift, it wouldn't have surprised her.

She carefully untied the string and opened the brown paper to reveal a box. She lifted the lid and unfolded a piece of lace wrapped around an iron crucifix.

Holding the box up so Mammi could also see, Elisabeth asked her uncle, "Did you make this?"

"Of course I did," he said, condescension back in his voice.

"And you made the lace," Elisabeth said to her aunt. The expression on her aunt's face told Elisabeth her aunt thought it a stupid statement: of course she had.

Elisabeth pushed down her pride: today was not the day to start an argument. "They're both beautiful. Thank you."

And she meant it.

CHAPTER THREE

Two suitcases lay open on Mom and Dad's bed: one for Juliana and one for Mom. Dance costumes hung on the closet door, with a list and an accessory bag attached to each hanger.

"Excuse me," Juliana said as she passed Opa, who was observing the packing ritual from the doorway. She grabbed her pyjamas, slammed the drawer shut and returned, tucking them into her suitcase. She then went to get her garment bag. "Excuse me again."

"What are those?" Opa asked as Mom lifted the costumes one by one off the closet door and placed them into the garment bag.

"My costumes," Juliana said, smiling proudly. She loved the costumes at this studio much more than those at her old one: the materials shone so beautifully, and the decorations sparkled more. But Mom had mentioned at the last competition that the costumes at Kitchener Dance Academy were much more expensive.

Opa reached for the one in Mom's hand—a black bodice with wispy silver accents sewn randomly around it. The broad shoulder straps flowed into a v-neck while the bottom of the bodice extended into bike shorts. Long, black gloves were in the accessory bag.

"That's very shiny for an undershirt," Opa said. "Where's the rest of the costume?"

Juliana laughed, but Mom didn't: the look on her face said Opa was experiencing another blip.

"Tata, dance costumes look like this. Don't you remember?"

Opa furrowed his eyebrows. "This is a costume? Juliana can't go to the dance in this. She'll never meet a good boy that way."

Juliana sighed. *Here we go again*, she thought sadly. For whatever reason, some of Opa's blips included concerns about Juliana's lack of a prospective husband even though she was only fourteen. It seemed almost as important to him as his other memories of Semlak. Boyfriends were so far from Juliana's mind that she always got her back up when Opa made comments like this.

Mom's voice sounded tense, but Juliana could tell she was trying to remain calm, just like the counsellor had told them to do.

"We're going to a dance competition, like what I used to do. The point isn't to find a husband, it's to show off how well you can dance. These aren't polkas and waltzes—the dancers kick and jump and do tricks. They need something that fits tight. You can't do a cartwheel in layers of underskirts." Mom took a deep breath and let it out.

"Ah..." Opa nodded. "Yes, you're right, Katy. Of course Juliana can't do all those wonderful steps in so many underskirts. She'd sweat too much."

Juliana smiled again. Not dancing in layers of underskirts so she wouldn't sweat was not the first reason to come to her mind, but it made sense.

But as she and Mom finished packing, Juliana began to worry: what if Opa said something like that in front of her new friends? Or got angry really fast at one of them? She'd seen his mood change quickly before. Or what if he started acting like he was back in Semlak? The counsellor had said that the family should do their best to acknowledge Opa's world and not to tell him he was wrong. But she didn't want to make a mistake worrying about him while she was onstage: she'd worked really hard these past few weeks to get better. Juliana felt guilty for thinking that, but it was true.

"How do you remember all those steps?" Opa asked the next afternoon. Juliana had changed into dance clothes immediately after finishing her homework and had started to practise. She did not want to mess up this weekend. "When we danced," Opa continued, "we always danced with partners and we did the same steps over and over. It looks like your feet are doing something different all the time. But it's so blurry, I wonder if I need new glasses."

Juliana laughed. She was getting used to his "old people" sense of humour. Sometimes he joked about his knees or his back. Today, his eyes held centre stage. "Well, it kind of is and it kind of isn't. I can really only hit the floor in a few different ways with my shoes." She demonstrated the different angles at which the two taps on each of her shoes could make contact with the floor and produce a sound. "But then I just combine those into something bigger. Like a shuffle." Juliana gently kicked her foot forward and then back, keeping her thigh fairly still and moving her lower leg enough that the tap on the ball of her foot touched her tap board in both directions. "You see?"

Opa burst into laughter. "The Schuhmacher Shuffle!"

Juliana laughed again. Opa was in a really good mood today. Juliana's last name was Roth, but her mom's maiden name was Schuhmacher. Opa had told her before about how his friend Karl had made fun of the way Opa walked, calling it the Schuhmacher Shuffle.

"I can't wait to watch you this weekend," Opa said.

"I hope I do better this time. Last time, one of the judges kept picking on me. It was kind of embarrassing."

"Then he was just being mean. You are a beautiful dancer and you practise a lot. More than your mom did."

As sweet as Opa's comment was, he seemed to have forgotten what dance competition was about. It was a judge's job to point out mistakes. Only the last time, the judge had done it too often. Miss Denise said a dancer needed to separate the good suggestions from the bad ones, but Juliana believed they were all good. She was the worst one in the group, after all. That meant she had a lot to improve on.

The creaking staircase caught Juliana's attention and she turned around to see Mom coming into the rec room.

"There you are, Tata," Mom said. "It's time to go to the club."

Opa looked momentarily confused, but then he remembered. "No, I'm going to stay here and watch Yulika," he said. "You were right, Katy. Her dancing is wonderful!"

Mom smiled and nodded. "It is, isn't it? But you and I have to go. Your friends are waiting for you there."

Opa shook his head. "I'm not going."

Mom's smile looked strained. "You also enjoy spending time with your friends. Besides, it's good for you. The doctor said to make sure you get out."

Again, Opa shook his head. "Yuliana, can you show me again those steps for *backofa*?" *Backofa* was German for *oven*. The first drawing in Omama's book was that of a simple kitchen that had no electricity, with the oven and stove built into the wall. Opa had told her about the *backofa* and how it had also heated the room behind it. Juliana had liked how the word sounded and had once choreographed a short tap combination to it. But now Juliana felt a bit awkward because Opa wanted her to keep dancing but Mom wanted Opa to leave so he could spend time at the German club with his friends.

"Katy, you should see this. She took a German word and made a dance to it."

Mom's smile drooped. She crossed her arms over her chest. "Tata, we have to go."

Opa stood up and the wrinkles between his eyebrows deepened. "Katy, your family has finally come home, and I want to spend time with everyone. I've seen the same friends almost every week for forty years. They can miss me once." Now he looked sternly at Juliana. "Do the dance again for me. I really like it."

When situations like this happened, Juliana still wished she were back home in Calgary: it seemed like no matter what she did here, somebody would get upset. In Calgary, Juliana either had only Mom at home, sometimes Mom and Dad, and occasionally just Dad. Whatever the configuration, Juliana's parents usually agreed with each other. *Even about punishments*, she thought. They never pulled her in separate directions.

Mom straightened her posture and drilled her eyes into Opa's. "Tata, I got someone at work to cover for me today so I could take you to your appointments this morning and then drive you to the club. They've got singers from Germany who'll only come to Kitchener this one time, and the club will be serving cabbage rolls and schnitzel. My colleagues at work changed a few things to accommodate us. Get a sweater and your coat and let's go."

Opa looked at Juliana's feet. "I want to watch Yulika dance more. She's fourteen and you've only now brought her to me. You can go back to work. I'm staying here." He looked expectantly at Juliana.

If she did what Opa asked her to, she'd make Mom angry. Although Juliana had no issues making Mom angry most of the time, she had also come to realize that this move had been hard on Mom, too. But Juliana also knew that Opa could get easily upset sometimes, and she didn't want that to happen now either.

"I'm getting kind of tired," Juliana said, deciding she should support Mom, especially because the counsellor had said that social time was important for Opa. "I think I'm going to take a break. Besides, you'll see me all weekend, and you'll see everything: the costume, the music, the stage..."

Opa wagged a finger at her. "You're siding with your mother." He tapped his skull. "This isn't that broken yet. I can tell what you're doing. I can still be smart like a fox sometimes." His voice made it clear that her decision had hurt his feelings.

Juliana's cheeks flushed. *It really doesn't matter what I do, does it?* she thought. *It's always wrong.*

"Tata, she's not siding with me. What she does takes a lot of energy. I know my daughter and I know she'll be practising even this weekend in between dances, right?" Juliana nodded. "Okay? You'll see her dance lots of times, but this evening you get to have your beer, sing whatever old songs they're singing, and have fun with your friends. Now, let's go."

Opa sighed and shuffled out of the room. Mom gave Juliana an exasperated look and followed him out.

Had Juliana done the right thing? If she'd continued dancing, she'd have made Mom mad. But stopping dancing had made Opa mad. And now she was mad because she'd been forced into that position in the first place. The counsellor had said that Alzheimer's patients changed their minds often, but it was important to help them stick to a schedule so long as that didn't cause them too much stress. Opa had written this evening's event on his calendar. It made sense to push him to go, but now he was angry with her.

What was Juliana supposed to do when she was caught in the middle like this? *I'm only fourteen,* she thought.

CHAPTER FOUR

*E*lisabeth hurried ahead of Mammi to the church, worried she was running late.

Maria, Elisabeth's best friend, ran toward her. "Lissika! There you are! I was worried you would go straight to the pastor's house before I'd see you!"

Elisabeth gave her a big hug. "I still have to get used to your bangs!" she said.

Maria and her family had travelled to Arad, their county's city, for several days, and Maria had returned with the hair at the front of her head cut short to just above her eyebrows.

"I already need to trim them," Maria said. "My hair is getting in my eyes."

Elisabeth laughed. "Mammi did say your hair would poke your eyes out."

Maria hooked her elbow into Elisabeth's and they began to walk toward the pastor's home, across the street. "Are you ready?"

Elisabeth sighed. "Just now, at Peter-Bátschi's house, I completely forgot how to ask Omama for forgiveness."

Maria's eyes popped open wide. "Did you do it, though?"

Elisabeth nodded. "Thanks to Anna. I guess she'd heard me recite those words often enough while I did housework. She got me started. But what if that happens during the public examination? Answering Pastor Fröhlich's questions in front of everyone frightens me."

Maria rubbed Elisabeth's upper arm. "I don't think you have anything to worry about. You've studied a lot for this. I've helped you and I know you know everything. Quick, what's Martin Luther's explanation of the…fifth petition in the Lord's Prayer?"

Elisabeth thought for a second and recited the answer perfectly.

"See?" Maria said, patting Elisabeth on the back.

"But you're one person, not hundreds of people!"

Maria gave Elisabeth a quick peck on the cheek. "Then pretend that we're back in your home studying and you're saying your answers only to me."

Elisabeth stopped and turned to face the church. The small, single-room yellow building with its lone steeple and empty belfry suddenly looked foreboding. Its two large wooden doors, currently closed, would soon open up to begin one of the most important events in Elisabeth's life. Even though Elisabeth had come here every Sunday since she was born, today she would be asked several questions in front of the congregation along with the other confirmands to demonstrate that she was ready to take responsibility for her relationship with God. By showing how much she believed and had learned, she would be able to receive Holy Communion, and at the end, she would become a *großmädchen*, one of the young, unmarried, confirmed women in the church. The boys would become *großbuben*.

But what if she dropped the host during communion? Or said the wrong words at the wrong time? She was glad she didn't have to be the one to speak on behalf of the confirmation class, the one who had to write and memorize a short speech that said the confirmands were taking leave of their parents and becoming responsible for their own actions.

"Stop worrying," Maria said. "You will be fine."

Elisabeth smiled at her best friend. "You're always so good at trying to lift my spirits."

"I know how important today is. I did this last year, and it was the best day of my life!" Maria's face broke out into a big smile. "But I didn't study half as much as you have. So, once again, Elisabeth Schuhmacher, *you will be fine!*"

Elisabeth squeezed Maria's arm with her other hand. *Thank you, Jesus, for such a good friend.* "Have you looked at my dress?" Elisabeth took a step back so Maria could see it better. "And my new shawl?" Maria gasped in astonishment as she took in Elisabeth's clothing. Elisabeth continued. "Mammi took extra time to prepare my dress for me *and* to embroider this shawl. She wants this day to be special."

"You're the first child to be confirmed in your family. Of course today is very special for her."

"And Luki even made sure my shoes were clean." Elisabeth pushed out one foot, showing her shiny but plain black satin slipper. Maria had begged Mammi not too long ago to make more modern designs, but Mammi was too busy repairing regular shoes in time for Easter to try something new. *Tata would have done that for me had he been here,* she thought. "I'm still nervous, though."

Maria turned Elisabeth to face away from the church and toward the church yard, where everyone else was still talking with their friends and family.

"Look, Lissika. You're not the only eldest child in the family here." She pointed out several of the other confirmands and Elisabeth saw her cousin, Little Sophie—so called because her mother was Sophie-Néni—one of the other eleven confirmands today. Seeing her immediately reminded Elisabeth of Andreas-Bátschi and Adam-Bátschi, Mammi's brothers who had died in the war. Within a few moments, Elisabeth saw their widows' new families. Elisabeth's eyes passed over the entire church yard, noticing all the missing fathers and brothers. Semlak had lost fifty-one men to that war, but more were missing today because Romania was still at war with Hungary. Thankfully, so far as she knew, there was little bloodshed in the Romanian-Hungarian war.

Elisabeth felt she had more in common with families whose father was missing—for whatever reason—than she did with the few who were the eldest in the family.

"Why are you suddenly sad?" Maria asked. "It's your special...ohhhh...Your father isn't here." Maria knew Elisabeth too well. Elisabeth nodded.

Like a cruel joke, Peter-Bátschi, his other three children, and Omama arrived just then. Little Sophie ran over to her father. He laid his hands on her shoulders, smiled, and said something to his daughter. The other Braun children began running around the church yard to find their friends.

"They are such wild animals," Maria said.

Elisabeth wanted to agree with her, but she couldn't rid herself of the small pang of jealousy she felt. Why hadn't her father waited one more year before leaving? Tata could even have left after Elisabeth's confirmation—he would've only had to wait another four months. And although Elisabeth hoped she would marry in the next year or two, she didn't know for sure if that would happen: Tata might choose to stay in America until she was engaged, or even a little longer. But at least he would have been here for today.

"Elisabeth!" Stefan waved his hat and rushed over to her.

A mischievous smile on her face, Maria said, "Oh, dear, I think I hear my mother calling me. I'd better go!"

Elisabeth shot Maria a look, and Maria grinned even more, though she kept her back to Stefan. Then she ran off.

To Elisabeth's relief, Georg and his brother, Samuel, and Georg's wife, Eva, were not far behind Stefan: they were slower because Georg only rushed if someone was in trouble, and Samuel limped because he'd had polio as a child. Eva didn't run because she was a married woman and it would have been improper.

"I wish you all the luck in the world today!" Stefan said. That he had been through so much because of the war and could still show such happiness made his joy contagious.

"Thank you." Elisabeth's cheeks became hot.

Georg and Samuel caught up. Samuel also gave Elisabeth a hearty hello, and this time Georg said hello, too, though only loud enough for Elisabeth to barely hear it.

Eva, by contrast, exclaimed, "Lissika! What a special day for you!" She and Elisabeth kissed on both cheeks. "You must be so happy!" Not old enough to wear only black, like their mothers did, Eva was dressed in dark blues and blacks from the headscarf on her head to her feet— except for her socks—the lack of colour contrasting starkly with the bright personality she showed in public.

"You'd better pass today," Samuel said playfully. "Lissi

and I had to get up extra early so we could be here on time." Samuel's wife was also named Elisabeth as were many other women in the church. He called her Lissi, but everyone else in the congregation called her Deaf Lissi. An ancestor of hers had been deaf, and the nickname had been passed down through the family. Samuel's wife could hear just fine, though.

"Now I'm even more nervous," Elisabeth said with a laugh.

"You'll do fine," Stefan replied. "You've been studying very hard."

Elisabeth saw the other confirmands heading across the street to the pastor's house, where they were to all meet beforehand. She excused herself and ran to catch up with them.

THE ORGAN PLAYED THE FIRST NOTES OF THE PROCESSIONAL hymn and Elisabeth's stomach rose into her throat. She swallowed to push it back down but was having very little success. Pastor Fröhlich looked at the line of twelve fourteen-year-olds behind him, nodded sternly, and turned back to face the congregation.

Wagner Anni suddenly whispered in her ear, "I've forgotten what I'm supposed to say!" Wagner Anni was to speak to the entire congregation on behalf of this year's class.

Elisabeth smiled at her and passed on Maria's advice: "You'll be fine."

Pastor Fröhlich whipped his head around, shushed Elisabeth, and immediately her cheeks burned.

"Thank you," Wagner Anni said as Pastor Fröhlich began his solemn walk down the aisle with the confirmands following behind him.

As the music filled their church and Elisabeth followed the procession, her nerves began to settle. She prayed to Jesus to help her pass so she could be confirmed.

She looked to her right and saw Mammi and Margarethe-Néni, their faces solemn. But...Elisabeth couldn't tell if she had seen properly. Was that a tiny smile coming from Mammi? Elisabeth chose to believe it was.

To her left sat the men. The rear half of the pews faced the altar, and this was where Samuel, Georg, and Stefan sat. Peter-Bátschi sat in this area, too. Samuel and Stefan grinned at Elisabeth.

Georg, though, sat pressed into the corner between the church wall and his pew, his eyes staring off into the distance. Elisabeth had seen him stare like this before, as though he were momentarily lost between heaven and earth. *Or even hell*, she thought, now that she better understood what the war had done to him. So far as she knew, the staring had never led to any fits. Hopefully it wouldn't today for his sake. She made eye contact with Stefan and then indicated her head toward Georg beside him. Once Stefan noticed, he whispered to Georg, and Georg's eyes turned in Elisabeth's direction, but he looked through her and not at her. She said a little prayer to Jesus to help Georg come back to his family from wherever he was right now. As she finished passing the rear half of the men's section, she caught Peter-Bátschi whispering to a man next to him and pointing at Georg. Peter-Bátschi and the other man laughed to themselves, and Elisabeth had to take a deep breath to stay calm.

The front half of the men's side was filled with pews facing the women. Konrad-Bátschi sat here. His face remained still and stern, though he did give Elisabeth a slight nod, which surprised her.

Elisabeth now passed the front rows of the nave, where the elders sat. On the right, with the women, was Omama, whose usual crotchety self was nowhere to be seen; she smiled at Elisabeth as her granddaughter passed by. Today was indeed a special day.

Elisabeth followed the line to the row of pews beside and facing the altar. If she succeeded today, she would sit here from now on. Maria and the other *großmädchen* and *großbuben* stood behind the confirmands. Elisabeth quickly made eye contact with her best friend, and Maria shook her clasped hands as a sign of excitement and encouragement.

With the processional hymn coming to an end, Elisabeth looked up to the balcony and immediately wished she could be sitting up there. Luki was poking Anna, who was attempting to swat him back while still looking like she was behaving, and Rosina had a finger up her nose. Elisabeth tried to make eye contact with them to tell them to stop, but they weren't looking in her direction. To her relief, one of the older children intervened.

Pastor Fröhlich took his position in front of the congregation and welcomed everyone. "Today is a very special day in our congregation. Not only do we celebrate Jesus's entry into Jerusalem, but we also celebrate two years of study by these young people. This year's confirmands, by the grace of God and their own hard work, will succeed and become adults in the church." He turned to face Elisabeth and the others. "Becoming an adult in our church means that you take responsibility for your faith: you live God's Word and deepen your relationship with Him every day. No longer can you rely upon your parents and godparents and grandparents to help you. They most certainly will if you ask, but the responsibility is now yours."

As Pastor Fröhlich continued to speak, Elisabeth tried to listen, but her mind was rushing through everything she had studied before. *What is the second commandment? Thou shalt not take the name of the Lord thy God in vain. What does this mean? We should fear and love God that we may not curse, swear, use witchcraft, lie or deceive by His name, but call upon it in every trouble, pray, praise, and give thanks. What are the first five books of the Bible? Genesis, Exodus, Leviticus, Numbers, Deuteronomy. Who are the twelve tribes of Israel? Reuben, Simeon, Levi, Judah, Issachar, Zebulun, Dan, Pahtali, Gad, Asher, Joseph, and Benjamin.*

Elisabeth's stomach was back in her throat.

"I still don't remember what I'm supposed to say!" Wagner Anni whispered in her ear, pulling Elisabeth out of her thoughts.

Elisabeth felt sorry for her: falling and breaking her nose earlier this year had caused Anni's nose to become crooked and had earned her the nickname Crooked-Nose Anni. As important as nicknames were to the Germans, that was one Elisabeth would not use. But if Anni forgot her words now, she might be given a worse nickname, one that might stick through the generations, like Deaf Lissi's. Better Crooked-Nose Anni than Dumb Anni.

Because Anni had practised in front of the confirmands for the past three weeks in confirmation class, Elisabeth knew how the speech began. She whispered the first words in Anni's ear. Anni's shoulders relaxed. She lifted her chin and stepped out in front of the congregation.

"On behalf of my friends today," she said, "who stand here before our church, our pastor, and God, I thank all of you for helping us learn about our faith and how we may deserve the grace of God and of His only Son, Jesus Christ."

Elisabeth saw Anni's mother and father in the crowd. Both nodded along as she recited her practised speech.

"You have taught us how to follow Jesus's teachings," Anni continued, "remember the will of God in all that we do, and to reject Satan. We now bid you farewell, as we take leave of your care and prove that we have learned what you have all taught us."

Sweat trickled down Anni's temples and she wiped it away when she sat back down. Elisabeth was relieved that she didn't have to give the speech. She felt better again.

Then Elisabeth realized that the reason she hadn't been chosen for that special moment was because she wasn't the best in her confirmation class. If Anni had had a hard time remembering her speech *and* she was the best in their class, that meant Elisabeth could make a mistake in front of everyone...

Pastor Fröhlich stood in front of the confirmands, folded his hands in front of him, and looked each person in the eye.

"Today is the day you will have the opportunity to share that you understand what it means to develop a relationship with God and to follow His Word and Jesus's teachings. For as you have learned, the first commandment says, 'Thou shalt have no other gods before me.' That we believe in God and only God is so important that it is the first commandment He gave to Moses. But what does it mean?"

He pointed to Little Sophie, who answered confidently, "We should fear, love, and trust in God above all things."

Pastor Fröhlich nodded. "You cannot have doubt in God or in Jesus's teachings," he said, "for they have stood the test of time and guide us in our lives today."

Little Sophie's younger siblings waved from their spots in the balcony, making Elisabeth embarrassed that she was related to them. But when she saw Peter-Bátschi smiling at his oldest daughter, her embarrassment turned to envy.

"What are the remaining nine commandments?" Pastor Fröhlich asked and pointed to nine students, stopping at Elisabeth on the fourth commandment—honour thy parents—and each one answered correctly.

Elisabeth remembered Tata's favourite saying: *Jesus is watching.* Sometimes the words sounded like a threat but often Tata meant them as comfort. Elisabeth was certain that Jesus was looking down on the congregation today; it was such an important event. As honoured as she felt about Jesus's presence, her realization caused her to begin rubbing her hands together.

Jesus is watching... Elisabeth sometimes wondered if others remembered that as often as she did: when she had witnessed a crowd ridiculing Georg, were they thinking about Jesus? When Pastor Fröhlich had chanced upon that crowd, many had tried to quietly sneak away without so much as apologizing to Georg. Even Peter-Bátschi had taken part and then slithered away like a snake.

She pulled her attention back to the pastor. And not too soon, either.

"Elisabeth?" Pastor Fröhlich said. "What is the story of Isaac?"

Elisabeth took a deep breath and explained how Abraham was told by God to sacrifice his son as proof of his devotion to God. After laying Isaac down on the altar and raising his knife, Abraham saw a messenger of God who told him to stop because he had proven himself faithful.

Pastor Fröhlich nodded and Elisabeth let out the rest of her breath. She had done it! She looked toward Mammi, who nodded with approval. She then looked to the right for Tata...

He's not here, silly, she thought. He would never see how well she had retold the story of Abraham and Isaac. Her heart sank. *That means I need to draw this in my book so I can show him when he returns*, she thought. But how? She certainly wasn't going to draw a picture of herself—a girl shouldn't boast. Her thoughts soon drifted to the empty seats on the men's side of the nave. Very few of the men were Georg and Stefan's age. The unmarried *großbuben* sat behind Elisabeth, any eighteen-year-old men were doing their military service, and many of the remaining men looked to be over forty. Still more were missing because they had travelled to America to search for work. Although Elisabeth knew her father was not the only one absent, he was the only one to leave the family with so little help. The parents of the Bartolf children who lived on the corner, for example, had both gone to America, but the grandparents looked after the children. There was certainly Maria's grandmother's cousin who was—

"Elisabeth?" Elisabeth jumped in her seat as Pastor Fröhlich now looked sternly at her and repeated the question he had just asked her. "What is the second petition of the Lord's Prayer?"

Her cheeks burning, she replied, "Thy kingdom come."

"And what does this mean?"

She recited from memory the passage in Martin Luther's *Small Catechism*: "The kingdom of God comes indeed without our prayer of itself, but we pray in this petition that it may come unto us also."

"And how is this done?"

The words now collected in her mind, they rushed out before she forgot a single one: "When our Heavenly Father gives us His Holy Spirit so that by His grace we believe His holy Word and lead a godly life here in time and hereafter in eternity."

The pastor nodded and raised an eyebrow, silently warning her to not let her mind wander again. He moved on to other students. Elisabeth didn't look at Mammi.

The service continued with the celebration of confirmation and Palm Sunday. Elisabeth received communion for the first time, and her blessing from the pastor for having passed, as did all the other eleven! As everyone stood up to sing the last hymn of the service, joy soared out of Elisabeth's heart and throughout the church, from the nave to the balcony and up to God. Looking at her siblings and Mammi, Elisabeth saw only smiles, and for a moment, she was certain she saw Tata smiling back at her, too.

CHAPTER FIVE

When Juliana opened the door to the hotel room, her mouth dropped. Beyond the foyer, the room expanded into two: the main living area, complete with a couch, queen-sized bed, armchair, and desk; and a separate bedroom with a king-sized bed connected to the ensuite.

"*Gott im Himmel!*" Opa exclaimed, clapping his hands to his cheeks. "How expensive was this, Katy?"

Juliana didn't care: the room was awesome.

"It's a standard room at this hotel," Mom said. "A lot of hotels these days are going this direction, and this one is newer."

All three squeezed through the foyer and Opa immediately put his suitcase on the couch. For a moment, Juliana wondered if she and Mom actually got the massive, king-sized bed. However, Mom corrected that in two seconds.

"Tata, you're sleeping in the master bedroom."

Opa stared at his daughter in amazement. "That bed is for me? Katy, I don't need such a big bed. I can sleep on a smaller bed."

Juliana heard Mom take a breath. The one-hour drive from Waterloo to Toronto had actually been quite pleasant. However, once they had entered Ontario's capital, something changed. It was as though Opa was seeing the city for the first time although Mom kept talking about the different trips they had taken as a family to the big city, getting agitated that Opa didn't seem to recall the trips. Opa's memories came back, but Mom's agitation never fully left.

"Like I said, this room is standard. It's easier for hotel staff to change one queen-sized bed than it is to do two single beds," Mom explained.

"This is too expensive, Katy," Opa said. "Can we get another room?"

Mom threw her suitcase next to Opa's. Juliana couldn't tell if Mom had thrown it because she was angry or because it was heavy.

"I'm sure the hotel is fully booked this weekend," Mom said. "We can't get another room."

"Then I'm going to pay you back for my part of the room," said Opa. "I can't let you pay for this for me."

Mom yanked Opa's suitcase off the bed and rolled it behind her into the master bedroom. She placed it on the luggage rack in the closet and opened it up.

"Your clothing will stay in here," she said. "And the bathroom is over here." She beckoned to Opa to follow her, and Juliana followed behind him. As Mom showed Opa how everything worked, Juliana's nerves tingled and she jumped up and down to shake her anxiety out. On the one hand, she was excited because her dancing had improved and she was sure she would perform better this time. On the other hand, she worried Opa's unpredictable behaviour might embarrass her.

Be nice, she scolded herself. *You know what the counsellor said: he can't help himself, even though he really wants to.*

"I can't wait to see you dance, Yulika," Opa said. "With a beautiful hotel room like this, you'll be able to sleep well. Sleep is really important for young people." He turned to face his daughter again. "But Katy, I know you and Peter and Annie are saving money for my care. You can't afford this hotel room. Had someone told me how expensive this would be, I would have stayed home."

Mom crossed her arms, took a deep breath and let it out, something she normally did *after* she was done being mad. However, Mom was becoming angrier, not calming down. "Tata, stop it. You wanted to see Juliana dance—you said yesterday it was really important for you to support your family—and we want you to see her, too. If you really enjoy it, we can certainly bring you along more often. Just stop complaining about the cost."

Opa pulled his shoulders back and looked his daughter square in the eye. He then responded in German.

When he finished, Mom said, "You keep saying how important family is to you, so here we are."

Opa replied again in German.

"We can afford this. Trust me: This is the cheapest part of the competition. Stop worrying."

Opa spoke louder when he responded, still in German. Juliana didn't know what he was saying but she could hear the stubbornness in his voice.

"Tata," Mom said, completely exasperated now. "We're not going to waste time driving back and forth! Juliana has an early morning on Sunday, and I don't want to risk getting stuck in traffic! Please! For once in your life stop worrying about how much everything costs!"

As the argument continued—Opa in German and Mom in English—Juliana's fists balled up in frustration. Didn't Mom see that Opa didn't understand? Mom was losing her patience with Opa really fast, when the counsellor had told them several times to do the exact opposite, to show him patience. But if Juliana said anything, that would make Mom angry, when now was probably not the right time to do that. Besides, Opa seemed to be fighting back on his own just fine.

Not knowing how to help—and feeling she probably

shouldn't even intervene—Juliana slid out of the master bedroom and sat in the armchair by the sliding door to the patio. She pulled out her phone, stuck in her earbuds, and scrolled through her social media feeds as she tried to drown out Mom and Opa's shouting. She understood that coming home to live with Opa was hard on Mom, but at the same time, Mom had wanted them to all move. So why was she arguing with Opa like this?

THE DANCE COMPETITION TOOK PLACE AT A THEATRE ACROSS the street from the hotel.

"Are my eyelashes straight?" Juliana asked Jasmine.

Jasmine scrutinized Juliana's eye makeup and false eyelashes and nodded. She pointed to Juliana's lips. "But you missed a corner with your lip liner."

Juliana touched up her lips, cleaned up her dressing area a little and realized she had forgotten her bag of snacks for the afternoon. She told Jasmine where she was going and searched for Mom and Opa in the theatre's lobby.

"Mom!" Juliana called across the lobby.

Mom turned.

"I'm really sorry, but I left my snacks in the hotel room. Can you get them for me?"

Mom placed her hands on her hips and raised an eyebrow. "Pardon?"

"Please?"

"Katy, who is this? And why is she asking you for snacks?" Opa asked.

Juliana's heart almost stopped. Had Opa's Alzheimer's progressed this fast?

Mom laughed. "Tata, this is Juliana. You just don't recognize her because of all her stage makeup."

How did Mom know when Opa was having a blip and when he was normal?

Opa stared at Juliana and Mom signalled to her to smile. Juliana did and saw recognition dawn on Opa's face. He even slapped himself on the forehead. "*So uh dummer Esel!*" he said. "I remember when your mom's teacher told me and Oma what kind of makeup she had to wear. Oma was horrified."

This conversation was getting even more confusing now. Why would parents be horrified about stage makeup? Although Juliana didn't care much for makeup during the day—it was too much work—she loved it for the stage. Sometimes Opa just didn't make sense, even when he was having a good day.

"You don't have to say any more," Mom said to him. "There are young kids around."

Juliana had a hard time believing that the few young

kids who were clinging to their parents were listening in on their conversation. But the expression on Mom's face said it was more of an excuse than a real reason to keep Opa from saying anything more.

"But first," Mom said, changing the conversation, "let's take a few pictures."

She pulled out her phone and Opa remarked that he still couldn't believe that such a tiny device took so many pictures. "When your mom was your age," he said, "cameras made a lot of noise, only took twenty-four photos, and then you had to pay to get the film developed."

"And sometimes wait for up to a week," Mom added. "Thankfully, times have changed."

"Yes, they have!" Opa said.

Mom instructed Juliana and Opa to stand next to each other for a few photos.

Jasmine came out to get Juliana, but before they left together, Juliana asked her friend to take a few photos quickly of her, Mom, and Opa.

As Juliana and Jasmine ran back to the dressing area, Opa called after her, "Good luck, Yulika!" Juliana waved back and breathed out a sigh of relief: Opa was indeed having a good day.

"Now!" Mackenzie said and all twenty-five dancers stood up in unison. "Now!" she said again and all dancers turned to the left, waited a beat, and ran off the stage together. Backstage, dripping in sweat, and huffing and puffing to regain their breath, all the dancers in Juliana's group came together in a group hug. On their way to the dressing room, Jasmine gave Juliana a big slap on the back.

"You rocked out there! You're on fire again, like that lantern in your great-grandmother's book!" Juliana had felt it, too. *My practice really is paying off*, she thought. She promised herself she would practise even more and decided that joining the dance club at school was a good idea. *I'll treat it like an audition*, she thought. *I'll learn those dances as fast as I can and then practise them at home.* Of course, no audition would give her time to practise the combinations at home. But that was beside the point. Joining the dance club would give her more chances to perform—even if it was just in front of a few dozen people—and learn new moves. If she ever wanted to audition, the experience would come in handy.

Backstage, among her costumes, accessories, and makeup kit, Juliana's phone dinged. She picked it up and grinned. It was a message from Dad:

Mom just texted that you were incredible on stage! High-five, sweetie! Your practice over March Break must have paid off!

Pride spilled out of Juliana's body. Her grin still on her

face, she held up her phone, gave a thumbs-up sign, and snapped a selfie to send back to Dad. She texted underneath, *Thanks! Only 3 more to go!*

Dad replied: *You can do it* 🤍

Juliana believed so, too.

CHAPTER SIX

*E*lisabeth swallowed hard. This was the first time in a long time that the extended Schuhmacher family sat together in their house: Konrad-Bátschi and Margarethe-Néni; Georg and Eva; Samuel and Deaf Lissi; Gretche and her husband, Michael Wagner; Susi and her husband, Adam Schubkegel; Mammi, Elisabeth, Anna, Luki, and Rosina.

The only one missing is Tata, Elisabeth thought. She almost wanted to insist that the chair at the head of the table stay empty but she knew she would be laughed at for such a sentiment. Plus, it would give her aunt and uncle another reason to complain about her father's absence. Instead, Konrad-Bátschi, as the oldest male family member, sat in that chair.

Anna carried a bowl of warm sauerkraut to the table

while Susi and Gretche brought over the goose, potatoes, and carrots. The adults sat tightly around the dinner table in the back room while Anna, Luki, and Rosina sat at the kitchen table.

"Konrad," Mammi said, "will you do the honours, please?" She pointed to the carving fork and knife.

Konard-Bátschi stood up and picked up the utensils. His face unmoving, he looked at Elisabeth and she worried that he would criticize her about something. "Today, we welcome you as an adult in the church," Konrad-Bátschi said. "This meal is in your honour, Elisabeth." Elisabeth shot a quick glance up at the crucifix and wondered if Jesus had anything to do with her uncle's friendly words. Konrad-Bátschi sliced into the goose and offered the first piece to Elisabeth. "I know my brother would have been very proud of you today."

Elisabeth questioned her hearing. Her uncle had said something kind. There was no sarcasm in his voice, and the expression on his face seemed genuine.

As Elisabeth's uncle continued to serve the goose, Mammi began passing around the boiled potatoes, boiled carrots, bread and butter, and sauerkraut.

Margarethe-Néni glanced at Mammi's belly. "Yes, it really is sad he's not here to celebrate such a momentous event." She accepted the carrots.

A gentle smile on his face, Samuel said, "I'm certain he's

working very hard for your family, Elisabeth, and is thinking of you today."

Elisabeth nodded in acknowledgement and silently said thank you to him.

"He chose to go," said Konrad-Bátschi. "Lukas knew today was coming and he chose to leave before Christmas."

Mammi rubbed her belly and drew her lips into a tight line but said nothing. Because Mammi's condition made her more irritable than usual, Elisabeth knew it would only be a matter of time before she defended her husband.

No one said anything further as the food made its way around. Elisabeth called to her siblings and asked them to bring their plates to get food. No sooner had her siblings returned to the kitchen than Konrad-Bátschi began again. "I understand that Stefan is building you a small heating stove in the workshop."

Mammi looked up from her plate and eyed her brother-in-law. Elisabeth admired Mammi's courage: she never backed down from Konrad-Bátschi. It had taken all of Elisabeth's courage to simply ask him and Margarethe-Néni for forgiveness this morning. Under no circumstances—especially today—did she see herself being bold enough to speak up to them for any reason, even if it were the right thing to do.

"The work that gets done around my house is none of your business," Mammi said directly.

Margarethe-Néni paid attention to her food as she

spoke. "We're only asking out of interest. We know you need the help with Lukas being away and not coming back for at least a year."

Samuel spoke up again. "Stefan is more than happy to help out. He says it will also show others that he can still work even with only one good arm, and it'll hopefully help him find paid work. It's wonderful that you've found something for him to do."

Konrad-Bátschi scoffed at his son's remark. "His missing an arm is no different than your limping because of that cursed polio. You're lucky Otata left me the *salasch* or you'd be in the same position."

Elisabeth wanted to throw her plate at her uncle. Why would he say such a thing to his son? Samuel could have learned how to make shoes, for example. That involved a lot of sitting. She again asked Jesus for forgiveness for her thoughts, but the anger Konrad-Bátschi had awakened in her still threatened to burst out.

The conversation continued with Mammi and Elisabeth's aunt and uncle arguing about Tata's absence, and Samuel occasionally trying to keep the peace. Gretche and Susi's husbands said nothing—which was to be expected, because Konrad-Bátschi was their father-in-law and they wouldn't have wanted to disrespect him. That none of the women spoke up also didn't surprise Elisabeth because it wasn't their place to do so. That left Mammi to defend Tata's decision by herself.

"So, Lissika," Margarethe-Néni said, turning to Elisabeth. "Now that you're old enough and confirmed, I'm sure you're looking forward to attending dances."

Elisabeth wasn't sure why the sudden change in subject, nor could she figure out the purpose of the question. But she had to be polite. She answered, "I am very much."

"Make sure that you dance with *großbuben* who don't plan to move away. It's very hard to raise a family by yourself."

Margarethe-Néni's underhanded comment made Elisabeth's blood boil.

"Elisabeth and her family only need the help for the year," Georg said, surprising Elisabeth. "Neither Samuel nor I have young children yet. We can afford the extra time."

Konrad-Bátschi banged his index finger on the table to emphasize a point, something most men did. "You should be helping me in that extra time. Your family must come first, not that of my brother's!"

"What if he doesn't return after a year?" Margarethe-Néni asked. "Will you still help his family when you do have young children?"

But Tata promised that he would return in a year! Elisabeth wanted to scream. *Tata will be home by next Christmas!* Her knuckles turned white as she gripped her fork and knife.

Georg didn't reply, but as the argument continued, a new realization disturbed Elisabeth: she agreed with her aunt and uncle. If Tata had stayed home, Elisabeth wouldn't need to worry about his safety or to ask Konrad-Bátschi's family for help. She would also have someone to continue teaching her from the encyclopedia set in the front room because she wouldn't be as busy looking after the household while Mammi continued Tata's business. But her aunt and uncle—whom Elisabeth had promised to honour—had again turned the conversation into accusations about Tata.

Her plate filled with food, Elisabeth stood up and excused herself, saying she had to go to the well to fill up the water jug.

"Anna can do that," said Mammi. "You are the guest of honour. You do not need to leave the table today."

"But I'm also an adult now in the church," said Elisabeth. "I should act like it." It sounded as good an excuse as any.

As Elisabeth walked around the table, she caught Eva's glance. Eva knew that Elisabeth wasn't telling the truth. Elisabeth prayed to Jesus for forgiveness as she stepped outside.

ELISABETH LEANED AGAINST THE WELL. HER PERFECTLY pressed, white skirt would get dirty, but she didn't care. Why would her aunt and uncle criticize her father's absence on such an important day? How could she tell the truth—that she agreed with them—without offending and insulting Mammi? She was angry at them for ruining her day, but she was also angry with herself for agreeing with the very comments that had ruined her day.

"They treat their sons so horribly," she said to Jesus, looking up into the sky. "I don't understand how I can have anything in common with them at all. And yet, suddenly, I do." As much as she wished God would send an angel down to her, her life was not a story from the Bible. To start with, neither God nor Jesus ever spoke to her. Sometimes she thought maybe God moved her heart in the right direction or influenced other people to make them act a certain way, but He never spoke to her in a way she could hear like He did for people in the Bible. And whenever she thought a miracle had happened—like the one time she believed Georg had been cured—it always turned out there had been no miracle.

The door to the house opened and Elisabeth stood up straight, expecting Mammi. She let out her breath when she saw that it was Eva walking toward her. Eva looked concerned.

"Is there anything I can help you with?" Eva asked.

Because Eva was only eighteen, she was more like a friend to Elisabeth than an older woman.

Elisabeth shrugged. How could Eva help? Tell her parents-in-law to stop being so mean? Ask everyone to not talk about Tata? Start the day all over again without Konrad-Bátschi and Margarethe-Néni there? What if they had become ill with a terrible cough this morning and were now at home resting?

"I don't know what to think," Elisabeth said. "Today is supposed to be about me but Konrad-Bátschi and Margarethe-Néni have made it again about themselves and my father. But at the same time, I can't help but agree with them. It would've been nice to have Tata home today." Eva nodded sympathetically as Elisabeth continued. "They are so mean to almost everyone, but especially to Georg, and yet I agree with them on this one point. What am I supposed to do? If I'm honest, the way we were taught to be in confirmation class, I would embarrass Mammi when I should be standing up for her."

Eva adjusted the shawl around her shoulders. Even though it was warming up outside, a cool spring breeze was blowing in from the east. "You're still Lissa-Néni's daughter. Sometimes it's not your place to speak up. That's just the way it is."

"But it can't be." Elisabeth sighed. "Why do they still despise my family so much when we really need their help right now?"

Eva didn't respond right away. When Eva wasn't around her family, she was a soft-spoken, quiet, and sometimes frustrated woman. It seemed wrong to Elisabeth that Eva had to behave differently at home in front of her husband's family.

"So many from our congregation have moved to Harrisburg. Just look at the Bartolfs on the corner," Eva said.

"But they don't pay their dues to the church and for their children's schooling," Elisabeth replied. "We still do."

"I don't think that matters. The fact that your father has left is what's important to everyone. His absence means others have to help."

Elisabeth turned the crank to lower the bucket into the well. "I wonder if life in the big city is this hard. How can everyone know everything about you if there are so many people?" The bucket plunked down into the water.

"The doctors might even know how to help Georg instead of spreading more rumours about him," Eva added.

"Stefan said another sanatorium has opened up in Arad." Elisabeth turned the crank and brought the pail back up.

"Or maybe in a big city people might spread rumours to more people," Eva said. "I don't know what life in a big city is like either."

Eva held the water jug for Elisabeth while Elisabeth poured water from the pail. The two were about to go back inside when Georg stumbled out of the house. He rammed his back against the wall, his body shivering, his eyes darting everywhere as though he was searching for an enemy. The door slammed behind him, but Elisabeth and Eva could hear Konrad-Bátschi still yelling at Georg through the closed door.

Dropping the water jug, Eva ran to her husband. Elisabeth followed but Eva held out her arm, keeping Elisabeth back.

"Sometimes he's so terrified that he thinks you're attacking him," she said. "The bruise on Tata's face was from yesterday. He has a much bigger one on his arm."

As Georg's fear turned to sadness, he began to sob. "No..." he said through his tears. He buried his face in his hands. "Why didn't you tell me?"

Elisabeth caught Eva touching her belly. "He's reliving the day he came home, isn't he?"

Eva nodded. "There's very little I can do to get him out of these nightmares." The sorrow on her face broke Elisabeth's heart. "He turns thirty in two days, and these fits show no sign of getting better. How will he be when our baby is born? Will he harm it? Will the baby remind him of everything he lost the first time?"

"Leave me alone!" Georg screamed and pushed his imaginary conversation partner away. Eva and Elisabeth jumped back, and Georg slumped to the ground, whimpering. "How dare you call me your friend! I hate you!" He sobbed, stamping his feet on the ground like a little child throwing a tantrum.

Elisabeth dared to look up and her worst fear was confirmed: people walking by were slowing down, and the woman who lived next door pretended to be tending to something at the front of her house, though her eyes were fixed on Georg. Elisabeth positioned herself better to block their view. *These wide skirts are at least good for something*, she thought.

Eva told Georg that everything was all right and that he had nothing to be afraid of, but he didn't respond. Stefan had told Elisabeth that Georg could only be coaxed out of his nightmare once Georg could hear those around him. Sadly, she and Eva had to watch as he shouted, screamed, and stamped for another few minutes before his awareness began to return.

"Georg," Eva said gently once he had settled again. "You have a new wife and you're expecting a new baby. Remember? These things make you happy."

Georg's face filled with confusion as he tried to sort out where he was. Eva turned to Elisabeth.

"I know my mother and father-in-law are horribly rude. But it is your day. You show so much courage when my husband is in trouble. Show a little courage for yourself, too. Don't let their rudeness ruin your confirmation." Eva's words took Elisabeth aback: Elisabeth had never thought of herself as showing *fear* about her own needs.

Eva took several cautious steps toward her husband and lay a hand on his shoulder. He nodded and placed his hand over hers. He wiped the tears from his eyes while Eva continued to speak softly to him. Sensing they wanted to be alone, Elisabeth refilled the water jug.

"If you need to go home," she said to Georg and Eva when she returned to the house door, "I'll certainly understand." She meant every word and fully expected them to accept her offer. Georg's temples were dripping with sweat and his face was as white as the clouds. Even though this fit was short, it still evidently tired him considerably.

But Georg shook his head as he tried to sit up and prop himself against the wall. "This is your special day," he said. Eva took out a handkerchief from his pocket and cleaned his face. "I am..." Georg took the handkerchief and wiped his eyes. "I am sorry for this." Georg lit a cigarette and breathed quickly in and out, as though the little burning stick would somehow calm him down.

Elisabeth couldn't bear to see him blame himself for these fits. She had come to realize—in part through Stefan —that Georg could not control this. Stefan had told her that thousands or maybe even tens of thousands of men who'd fought in the war had problems at home. He had told her about seeing some of these soldiers—some injured even more than he himself was—begging on the streets as he travelled through Russia and Eastern Europe on his return to Semlak. The stories were too difficult for Elisabeth to hear, but she knew one thing: Georg was not to blame for what was happening to him.

Unfortunately, except for Stefan and Eva, no one else agreed with Elisabeth.

Eva stroked her husband's cheek and held his hand. They exchanged glances again but Elisabeth had run out of excuses to give them more time alone. After another moment of silence and private looks, Eva spoke. "We would like to stay, Lissika, if that's all right with you."

The decision shocked Elisabeth. Wouldn't they rather go home and stay away from his father, if only for another hour or two? Elisabeth insisted they didn't have to stay.

Georg pushed himself onto his feet and Eva dusted off his suit to remove any dirt from the ground or white lime from the wall that had been rubbed into his clothing.

"Would you rather...we leave?" Eva asked, a touch of sadness in her voice.

Elisabeth panicked. That was the last thing she wanted them to think, especially because it wasn't true. "No, of course not! You can most certainly stay! I just want to make sure that you're...comfortable." She didn't know what to expect from Konrad-Bátschi when all three of them walked back inside together. The last thing she wanted for her cousin and his wife was further ridicule.

Georg breathed in deeply on his cigarette and let it out, his breathing now slowed down. "Your father left to provide for his family. He is a kind, honourable man. Do not let my parents tell you otherwise."

"But he could have found good-paying work in Arad or Temeswar," Elisabeth said, naming two big cities within their region.

"Men earn more in America," Georg said. "Much more. It is the land of milk and honey. My father would never survive there: to work with others from different countries, you have to try to understand them." He spat on the ground, the first real show of anger from him that Elisabeth had ever seen. "Tata can't even be nice to the Romanians or Jews here. What would he do in a country with so many races?" He dropped his cigarette on the ground, stamped it out, picked it up, and flicked it onto the street.

But his words didn't calm Elisabeth's growing anger. What good was all that money if her father wasn't here to celebrate such a milestone in her life? Why couldn't that money wait for a few more months? Or at least until after the winter wheat harvest and spring sowing?

If he had known that Mammi was expecting a baby, maybe he wouldn't have left at all, Elisabeth thought.

With everyone ready to go back inside, Elisabeth placed her hand on the doorknob, but she hesitated. "Are you sure?" she asked Georg.

"Don't worry about me," he replied. "This is your day."

Eva's words from a few minutes before—that Elisabeth

should show courage for herself—returned as Elisabeth opened the door.

"Look what the cat dragged in," Margarethe-Néni replied, rolling her eyes at her son.

"Finally decided to join us?" Mammi said to Elisabeth. She was clearing away the dishes, with Anna, Rosina, Margarethe-Néni, Gretche, and Susi helping her. "This is your day, Elisabeth, not Georg's."

Elisabeth's blood boiled again, but Eva's gentle touch on her back reminded her to stay calm. She begged Jesus for patience, apologized to everyone for her absence, and asked Mammi how she could help.

But Tata's presence would have certainly made today much easier. Elisabeth couldn't wait for the visit to be over.

ELISABETH SAT IN THE BACK ROOM, HER SHOULDERS HUNCHED over her sketchbook, while her siblings and mother sat in the front room, Anna and Mammi repairing clothing, Rosina knitting her scarf, and Luki playing with Tata's deck of cards.

Elisabeth began sketching Jesus's hair—she was copying the painting that hung at the front of the church, the picture of Jesus praying to His Father on the Mount of Olives. The sketch in her book was much smaller than the real painting, of course, especially because she also included the pulpit and several rows of pews, decorated in flowers. Although her aunt and uncle had angered her greatly during the celebratory meal, the confirmation itself had been an occasion of joy. That was what Elisabeth wanted to share with Tata in this drawing when he returned.

Normally Mammi would expect Elisabeth to help with mending that evening. But Elisabeth had taken Eva's words to heart and asked instead if she could draw, even for a little while. She didn't tell Mammi that it helped her feel better, just that she wanted to draw the picture for Tata as he had asked her. To Elisabeth's surprise, Mammi had agreed, though not without her usual comment about the futility of Elisabeth's artistic gift.

"I'm so happy for Anni," Elisabeth said to her sketchbook. "She was so nervous about her speech today, and yet she still found the courage to thank everyone on our behalf." After the ceremony, Elisabeth had made sure to offer her own thanks to Mammi and her siblings for their help.

As she shaded in Jesus's robe, Elisabeth had a marvellous idea.

"You used bread to feed the multitudes," she said to Jesus. "You also shared bread at your last supper. And when I invited Georg and Eva to our home that time he had had that horrible fit, I gave them bread and it made them feel better."

That was what she was going to do tomorrow. Saying thank you was important but giving a gift of thanks was even more important. She and her sisters would bake many loaves of bread to give to friends and family to thank them for their help. Elisabeth was not going to let her aunt and uncle ruin her day—just as Georg and Eva had told her not to. Instead, she was going to turn it into a day of thanks that would last for several days, until Green Thursday, when the final preparations for Easter would begin.

CHAPTER SEVEN

"Juliana," Mom said from the driver's seat. "It happens all the time. You really need to learn to let these things go."

"Be nice to her," Opa said. "You needed a long time to be happy again, too."

"Of course I did," Mom said defensively. "And I learned to get over it."

Mom's comments weren't helping. In the ballet group, Juliana had started the fouetté turn sequence on the wrong foot. She only noticed *after* her initial preparatory turn—which she had done in the wrong direction—when she extended her right leg forward, relevéed on her left foot, and carried her right leg to the side to second position. Thankfully, Juliana had been a split second early, which meant that her leg had reached second position just before

Jasmine's left leg did and Juliana could pull hers back in, preventing a painful and embarrassing crash.

In the end, Juliana had stood there in her tutu, as still as a tree amid her whirling friends.

Mom said, "I remember this one really embarrassing moment—"

"I don't care," Juliana interrupted. Nobody had videoed dance competitions back then and there was no social media when Mom had danced. Juliana hadn't opened her social media streams since the mistake occurred out of fear that someone would have posted it.

Her elbow perched on the door, Juliana rested her chin on her hand and stared out at the snowy world as it rushed by. Finally she saw a green sign that said King Street. They were almost home, thank God.

"You'll be fine," Mom said. "These are your friends. They understand."

Dad had texted the same to Juliana earlier after Mom had told him about it. What if she had accidentally sent that text to the wrong person? Then it would've taken all of two seconds to go viral. It could go that fast.

Juliana sighed. The chances of such a message going viral were actually pretty slim. But that didn't matter. What mattered was just how fast a mistake like standing still during a climactic fouetté turn sequence could spread.

I practised so hard, Juliana thought. *How could I make such a stupid mistake?*

"The mall looks so empty," Opa said. "Must be closed for the day." Opa looked at the clock on the dashboard. "That's strange. It should still be open."

"Sears closed down," Mom said. "Annie said they were tearing down the store and putting something new up, but she couldn't remember what."

"They closed Sears? They can't close Sears. That's where your *modr* bought all your children's clothes. They had good prices."

"It went bankrupt. Annie said it was all over the news for months."

Juliana looked up at Mom in the rearview mirror and saw a flash of sadness cross her face. Juliana guessed that Opa was supposed to know what was going on with this mall, but it meant nothing to Juliana. Buildings were torn down and rebuilt all the time. So what if Oma had bought Mom's baby clothes there? Juliana had no idea where Mom had bought hers. Juliana understood if Opa missed his hometown and his mother, but a store?

A pause in the conversation let Juliana's mind return to her mistake. She had enough space in Opa's rec room to practise those turns. The problem was that Juliana preferred to turn the other way, so it was a matter of getting used to turning the right way. She closed her eyes and imagined the sequence again, hoping to mentally rehearse it right now. But all she saw was herself standing still.

"Well," Opa said. "At least you can take Yulika to Sports-

World for some mini-golf once this snow finally melts. I could come, too. The doctor said exercise is good for me."

Mom didn't answer. Hadn't she heard him? Juliana opened her eyes and saw Mom's sad face. Opa must have again said something he wasn't supposed to.

"Do you like mini-golf, Yulika?" Opa asked Juliana.

"I don't know."

Opa looked accusingly toward Mom. "You've never taken her mini-golfing? Why wouldn't you continue that tradition?"

Mom flicked on her blinker and changed lanes. "We just never found the time."

Juliana knew it was an excuse and not the truth. Mom frequently said she didn't have time. *She only has one kid and one job*, Juliana thought. *How can she not have time? She's hardly looking after her dad as it is.*

"Then we will start the tradition again," Opa said. "When the snow finally melts, we'll all go to SportsWorld."

Juliana had no idea what SportsWorld was. And although mini-golf didn't exactly excite her, the thought of doing something outside the house with Opa sounded like fun. She had enjoyed Opa being at this competition. At times he got confused, and Mom had had to gently (and sometimes impatiently) remind him of where they were. But every time he saw Juliana in one of her costumes, his eyes were open wide and were sometimes even filled with tears. That much emotion made her uncomfortable. But the counsellor had said that emotions could come out faster in Alzheimer's patients.

Of course, Juliana didn't know what her grandfather had been like in the past. Mom and Dad had never flown back to Kitchener with her, and she was pretty sure Opa had never flown out to Calgary. Not that she remembered, anyway.

"Katy, you're not saying anything," Opa said. "Are you really that against tradition that you can't take us to Sports-World to go mini-golfing?"

Of course she is, Juliana thought. *She hasn't taught me anything about my family. I didn't know three of my grandparents, so why would I care about the only one still alive? Hmmm, maybe because it's actually nice to have a grandparent?*

But the look on Mom's face said something different: sadness mixed with hesitation. After a long moment, Mom finally spoke. "Tata, SportsWorld closed down several years ago. We already passed where it used to be."

"What?" Opa strained to look back.

"We passed SportsWorld Drive five minutes ago. You can't see it anymore. It's all stores there now."

"And Lulu's?"

"Long gone."

SportsWorld and Lulu's meant as much to Juliana as the closed-down store at that mall. In other words, nothing. But judging by the looks on Mom's and Opa's faces, they had been important places to them.

"No one told me," Opa said.

"Tata..." Mom looked like she was trying to decide whether she should keep talking. "You read and watch the news every day. You would've known."

Opa shook his head. "No, no one told me."

Mom nodded but not in agreement with Opa. Her nodding looked more like she was accepting defeat in the conversation.

If you'd brought us back more often, Juliana thought, her anger returning, *you could've made some of these memories with me and Opa.*

Juliana renewed her promise to spend more time with Opa, even if it meant sacrificing a bit of her practice time. She needed to practice more than she had, but just because Mom didn't want to spend time with Opa didn't mean that Juliana had to follow suit.

To Juliana's surprise, Opa wanted to try a piece of toast with sunflower seed butter and apple butter on it. "I think it's one of your favourite snacks?"

Juliana happily made two slices of toast: one for her and one for him.

"We were talking about the Rocky Mountains in school today," Juliana said. "No one in my class had ever seen them up close, so my teacher wanted me to describe them."

Juliana paused to see if Opa was following the conversation.

"I remember seeing them when we visited Katy once," Opa said. "They're like the Alps, right?"

Julia nodded. "So you visited Mom?" Her voice sounded hopeful. Maybe Opa had visited her and Juliana had simply been too young to remember.

"Your *oma* and I went out to visit Katy and Paul after they'd married, but it was before you were born." Opa shook his head. "Irmgard's Parkinson's eventually kept her at home. She was too embarrassed to go outside, even with friends. She wanted to see Katy more often, but Irmgard didn't want to be seen." Opa paused for a minute, lost in thought. "Her shaking head embarrassed her. She died a few years later, and then I didn't want to travel by myself." Opa shrugged. "I'm sorry. Maybe I should've tried harder, too. But Katy never invited us, and she never wanted to come back here."

Juliana felt a little embarrassed that her question had brought up such an unpleasant memory. Should she apologize?

Opa continued. "We didn't have mountains in Semlak. We lived in the valley. The Rockies are beautiful, but they felt scary, like big monsters."

Juliana smiled at the comparison. She could see how someone might think that.

"When I first moved to Kitchener," Opa said, "there

were so many trees. I had friends back then who lived in Stanley Park. That neighbourhood was new in the seventies and eighties. They had a hill behind them, and past that hill was a cornfield. You could even see Blue Springs from their backyard."

"Blue Springs?" Juliana asked.

"It was a little pond and a small beach. You could go swimming there. I took Annie, Katy, and Peter sometimes, and it was nice. But you could see so many trees. Now, when I see my friends at the club, they talk about how there's that road now, that the cornfield has turned into houses, and that you can't see the trees anymore because there are more houses there, too."

Truth be told, Juliana didn't really care about changes in Kitchener. The conversation was becoming boring.

"But that hill on King Street in Waterloo—to someone from Semlak, that's a mountain."

Waterloo was Kitchener's twin city. Anyone who lived here long enough called both cities K-W, because only signs told you there was a border. Juliana had even heard stories at school about the border travelling through some people's homes. But Juliana knew the hill Opa was talking about. It was just a regular hill on a street. It wasn't that big.

"Do you like it here?" Opa asked, biting into his snack again. He studied the toast as he chewed. "This is good," he said. "Almost like peanut butter. Your family is bringing new food into my home!"

Juliana smiled. Opa's observations often sounded like he was discovering the world for the first time. Some things were new to him—like this snack—but others clearly weren't, like when they drove by that mall in Kitchener.

"Well, I like living in your home," she replied to his question. "But I feel so, I don't know, exposed here. The Rockies...I felt like they were hugging me all the time." She shrugged, not sure if her explanation made sense. "I know they're a ways away from Calgary, but they felt like big arms hugging me. When I'm here...I don't know." She struggled to find words. Dancing these thoughts out would've been much easier. "I guess I feel like I can keep going and going and not stop. There's no final destination."

Opa laughed with understanding. "I have never thought of flat land like that." He paused as he chewed, and Juliana took the opportunity to bite into her own toast. "Yes, Yulika, you are right. But I still like that. It means that if I don't like where I am, I can easily go somewhere else."

Juliana could see his point of view, though she still liked the "hugginess" of the Rockies. It wasn't the word she had used when she described the Rockies at school, of course. Her classmates would've probably laughed at her for that kind of comparison. She wouldn't even tell her parents that—it was too weird somehow. But she could use the word with Opa. He understood and didn't think anything of it besides it being a good explanation.

"In English," Opa said, "you only have one word—

home. But in German we have *zuhause* and *heimat*. *Zuhause* is your house, your city, where you live. But *heimat* is where your heart lives. Even if you stay in Kitchener for the rest of your life, I think Calgary is your *heimat*. Kitchener is my home, but Semlak is my *heimat*."

That's why he always thinks of Semlak, she thought. *It's where his heart is.*

Exhausted after a hard practice session at home—as usual, the studio cancelled practice the night after a competition—Juliana got herself a tall glass of water in the kitchen and crashed on the couch in the living room. She had thought of something while she rehearsed and wanted to look it up on her phone. She opened the maps app and typed in "Semlak." It auto-corrected to "Semlac, Romania." Confused but assuming it was the same place, she clicked on it and the map flew to a small village in Romania. She noticed that the village was laid out mostly in a grid pattern along the north shore of a river, with three main streets running east to west. She asked the app for directions from Semlak to Harrisburg, Pennsylvania, where Omama's father had worked for a time. She watched the map zoom out and create a line across the Atlantic Ocean to the American city.

"What are you doing?" Opa asked as he came into the living room and sat next to Juliana.

"I'm just looking up how far Semlak is from Harrisburg," Juliana said. "But my phone changed the spelling. Is this the right place?" She held her phone out for Opa to see.

Opa nodded. "In Hungarian, it was S-Z-E-M-L-A-K. In German, S-E-M-L-A-K. And in Romanian, S-E-M-L-A-C. Your phone gave you the Romanian spelling. That's the one they use today." Opa took the phone out of her hand and studied it for a moment. "What's this?" His finger pointed at the line that stretched between Semlak and Harrisburg.

"This is a map on my phone and it shows me the distance between Semlak and Harrisburg. It's twice the distance as from here to Calgary."

"Your phone can tell you that?"

Juliana nodded.

Opa peered out at his rotary-dial phone in the kitchen. "I wish my phone would tell me those kinds of things."

Juliana thought back to an unfinished letter from Omama to her father that she and Sophie had found in those ancient encyclopedias in the basement. Uncle Peter had sent Juliana and Sophie a translation of the letter. "When I see how Omama had to write letters to her father to talk with him, and then I see how far that letter had to travel, suddenly Calgary doesn't seem so far away."

Which meant that Rachel was closer to Juliana than Omama's father to his daughter. She took her phone back from Opa and looked up the time difference between Romania and Pennsylvania: seven hours. The time difference between Kitchener and Calgary was only two hours. Not to mention the fact that Juliana could text Rachel, call her, or send her an email, and know that Rachel would see it by the end of the day.

"It's like I said before," said Opa. "Calgary is your *heimat*."

Normally, Juliana would take advantage of times like this to ask Opa about his family. And usually, Opa would interrupt the conversation when he suddenly remembered something he had to do, like calling a friend. But this time, Juliana's heart was longing for Calgary.

"I hope you don't mind, Opa," she said as she stood up. "I'm going to call Rachel. It's her March Break this week. She should be home."

Opa patted Juliana on the hand and smiled at her. "Of course not, Yulika. It's easier to keep in touch with your friends these days, so you have to try. Friends are almost as important as family."

CHAPTER EIGHT

*E*lisabeth had awoken early the following morning to mix a large amount of sourdough in a wooden bread trough made out of a carved-out tree trunk. Every household had such a trough: it allowed the women and girls of the house to knead enough dough to bake many loaves. A mixture of flour, water, yeast, and salt, plus sourdough from the last baking, the floury paste had rested for half the day. Now early afternoon, Rosina, Anna, and Maria were preparing to knead it into bread dough.

"Thank you so much for helping us today," Elisabeth said to Maria. "I hope you'll take a loaf home when we're done. You have helped us a lot, and I don't know how else to thank you."

After Elisabeth had finished her morning chores, she and Rosina had gone to the store to buy yeast. On their way home, they had bumped into Maria. When Elisabeth told her about the idea, Maria asked if she could join her. Of course Elisabeth said yes.

Maria squeezed Elisabeth's arm. "I know how hard it is for your family with your *tata* away. We have help at home, and with the farmhands' wives cooking and baking their own food, Mammi and I only have to cook and bake for the four of us. It means I have a little extra time to at least help you with the kneading. Give the bread to others." She giggled. "You could even give one to Herr Meier for bringing his boots to your mother."

Herr Meier was the village gossip. He disapproved of how much Georg and Samuel were helping Elisabeth's family. The thought of surprising him with a loaf made Elisabeth laugh. But silently, she promised herself that she would embroider Maria a handkerchief later.

Together Elisabeth and Maria hoisted a new sack of flour onto a chair and Elisabeth sliced it open with a knife.

"What do you think about Hagel Konrad as a husband?" Maria asked. Konrad had once helped around the Schuhmacher home with his father, Hagel Samuel, who was Sophie-Néni's brother. (Elisabeth had never tried to prove it, but with the first Lutheran Germans only arriving in Semlak in 1819, and almost no one marrying outside of the church, she was certain almost everyone was related to everyone else somehow.)

Rosina didn't wait to be asked for her opinion. "He doesn't listen to his father."

Elisabeth admonished Rosina for her comments, but Rosina insisted they were true. "Herr Hagel yelled at him that he wasn't helpful," she said.

Maria smiled at Rosina's honesty. "But don't forget," she said, "people do learn from their mistakes. By now he may admit that he was wrong."

He would never do that, Elisabeth thought. Hagel Konrad was too proud.

Elisabeth asked Anna to heat some water. Anna took a large pot off the stove and headed outside without arguing. Maria's visit meant Anna would probably behave. That Anna had allowed her to tie her apron proved that. Anna usually only argued with Elisabeth or fought with her when others weren't around.

Elisabeth and Maria used bowls to scoop flour into the trough.

"I'm sorry," Elisabeth said, "but I don't like him. Mammi and Omama say that a good man is one who looks after and protects his family and apologizes when he's made a mistake. Remember that day he came to help with our pig stalls?"

Maria nodded.

"Konrad didn't apologize, even after it was clear that his mistake had led to the pigs running loose."

Maria crumbled more fresh yeast into the trough. "But

a good marriage is also one where your husband has a trade and isn't just a farmer," she said. "I don't mean to insult your mother's family, but it is true."

Elisabeth understood what Maria was trying to say but almost all the men in their congregation worked as farmers. The Hagels, Konrad-Bátschi, Georg, Tata, and a few others were the exceptions. Among these, only Hagel Konrad did not have a wife. Chances were slim that Elisabeth would find a husband who practised a trade, but under no circumstances would she ever consider Hagel Konrad again. But Maria knew that so why was she asking?

Astonishment flashed in Elisabeth's eyes. "Are *you* considering him?" she asked Maria.

A sheepish smile appeared on Maria's face and Elisabeth tossed a tiny amount of flour in Maria's direction but only far enough that it would still land in the trough. "You're only telling me now?"

AT THE MORGANS' HOUSE, AUNT ANNE HUNG HER TABLET ON its perch on the fridge door. "The last time I tried baking bread was...oh, I don't even know when. When I was pregnant with Rebecca? But it came out as heavy as a brick, so I gave up."

Opa was sitting at the table in Aunt Anne's kitchen, a

coffee in hand. He laughed. "I'd forgotten—you couldn't bake in your younger years."

"Oh, don't remind me. Modr's 'this much of this' and 'that much of that' somehow just didn't work for me." She smiled at Juliana. "Once I discovered cookbooks and—" she gasped ironically— "*measuring cups*, I was golden."

Dean—who was the same age as Juliana—and Sophie stood at the ready in the kitchen next to Juliana. A heavy snowfall had begun by mid-morning, and by four o'clock, all evening activities had been cancelled. Aunt Anne had invited Juliana, Mom, and Opa over for some baking, but Mom had declined.

Aunt Anne checked the recipe one more time.

"A friend from the German club sent me this website," she explained. "Tata—what's her dad's name? You play cards with him." She looked at Juliana. "It's a really funny name."

"Whose?"

"Sara's dad's name."

Opa scratched his bald head and then it came to him. "Krummnase Adam." He translated for the kids: "Crooked-Nose Adam."

Juliana, Sophie, and Dean snorted.

"Why on earth...?" Dean asked, but he couldn't finish his sentence he was laughing so hard.

Aunt Anne explained. "It was his mom's name. She had fallen and broken her nose, and medical help being what it was back then, it stayed crooked. So that became her name."

Opa added, "Because so many people had the same name, you got a nickname. I think his mom's name was Anna." Opa looked mischievously at his daughter.

"My nose is straight," Aunt Anne said. "So, this website Sara gave me has lots of recipes from the old country." She sighed and placed her hands on her hips. "It's too bad your mom chose errands over this," she said to Juliana, sounding disappointed.

"Tell me about it," Juliana replied. She peeked over her aunt's shoulder, but the recipe was in German so she couldn't understand it. "Do you read German?" Juliana asked Sophie.

"Nope. Never learned."

"Me neither. It sounds, I don't know, kind of ugly."

Sophie giggled and Dean nodded in agreement.

"What's that?" Opa asked.

Juliana's cheeks turned red. "Sorry."

Opa shook his head. "Annie, you and your sister are not teaching the children."

Aunt Anne was looking for something in a lower cupboard. "That's why we're baking," she said and shot the kids a look to tell them to knock it off. She pulled out measuring cups with one hand and picked up a bag of flour with the other.

"Okay. I've got some sourdough starter here from Sara,"

Aunt Anne said, pointing to a small bowl on the counter. She then explained the steps of the recipe to everyone. Dean seemed to be the only one who looked excited about the task: he listened closely to his mother and watched her movements as she held up measuring cups and pointed to the mixing bowl.

Sophie leaned over to Juliana and whispered, "I'm surprised you came. I thought ripping lettuce would be more fun."

Juliana playfully poked her younger cousin in the ribs with her elbow. "Thanks for the vote of confidence! Actually, after the weekend I had, I needed some fun."

Aunt Anne said, "I heard about your ballet number." She crouched down by a cupboard to find something else. "Here it is! Yeast! The recipe calls for fresh yeast, but I'm going to use dry yeast instead. I found the conversion online."

She stood up, placed the small jar on the table next to the other ingredients, and nodded. She was ready. "So, it won't be too hard. And we're not doing it by hand, obviously. I just have to find my dough hook. Dean, have you seen it? I've never used it." She looked at Juliana again. "He wants to be a chef, so I taught him to bake the modern way."

Both Dean and Aunt Anne began opening up cupboard after cupboard in search of the elusive dough hook.

ELISABETH, HER SISTERS, AND MARIA PUSHED AND PULLED AT the large mass of dough in the trough.

"I can't wait to marry either," said Elisabeth. "But certainly not *him*. Besides, I have time: I want to make sure Tata is home for that day. He missed my confirmation. I don't want him to miss my wedding, too."

"Do you plan to marry within a year?" Maria asked. "You said your father would be gone only a year."

"No, but..." Should she talk about this while her sisters were listening? She hoped her siblings hadn't heard Margarethe-Néni's comment yesterday about Tata maybe staying longer, but she wasn't sure. "I'd like Tata to get to know him before we get married. And of course he has to give his permission."

"Who are you going to marry?" Anna asked her sister.

Elisabeth hesitated. Stefan was kind and helpful, and Elisabeth enjoyed talking to him about the wider world. She had taken a liking to him but she didn't want to say anything right now: Maria couldn't keep something like this a secret, while her sisters would annoy her about Stefan every time he came over.

"I'm not sure yet," she replied, her little lie accompanied by her usual request to Jesus for forgiveness.

"Weren't you interested in Stefan?" Maria said, obviously not understanding the intent behind Elisabeth's reluctance to say anything more. Both of Elisabeth's sisters stopped kneading and stared at her.

Elisabeth blushed. What could she say now? If she said no, Maria could possibly spread *that* rumour and Stefan would likely hear about it and believe it. If she said yes, she was in for a lot of teasing.

Just then, the door opened, and Stefan entered. All four girls stared at him, not saying a word.

Stefan paused at the unexpected silence. "Are you talking about me?" he asked jokingly.

"No," Elisabeth immediately answered.

Rosina glared at Elisabeth. "You're not supposed to lie!"

Could this get any worse? Elisabeth thought. Her cheeks burned as Stefan threw her a curious glance.

"Frau Schuhmacher would like a snack and some water," he said, regaining his composure, and he told Elisabeth what Mammi wanted.

Elisabeth used a cloth to wipe off the remnants of dough from her fingers and asked the girls to keep kneading.

Stefan was at the Schuhmachers to build Mammi a small heating stove in her workshop. Although the days were beginning to warm up, the evenings were still cool. The midwife had said at the beginning of the month that Mammi needed to rest during the day—she had been getting sick from working too hard. That meant Mammi had to work into the evenings instead of sitting in the front room with her children while the girls did handicrafts and mended clothing and Luki played.

Stefan took the plate of food and glass of water from Elisabeth and returned to the workshop.

Elisabeth glared at Rosina and then dug her fingers back into the dough and let the rest of her anger out through her hands.

"He is a nice man," Maria said. "And I can tell he likes you, Lissika. But one thing you should think about is that he's, well, missing an arm."

Elisabeth snorted at the statement. "That's obvious," she said. "But you gave me a comb so I would have something pretty to wear in my hair. And before my confirmation, you claimed—in the church yard!—that your parents were calling you, when they most certainly weren't. I don't think you think this is the worst idea."

Anna and Rosina both dropped their jaws. Elisabeth had to change the subject sooner rather than later. They were too young for this kind of talk about their oldest sister. "So," Elisabeth said to Maria, "you might be interested in Hagel Konrad? He still has to do his military duty."

Maria stared at the floor for a moment, and Elisabeth worried that she had offended her. She had meant her words as a fun jibe at her friend, not as an insult.

Maria took a deep breath and looked Elisabeth in the eyes again. "Hagel Konrad is proud. Maybe too proud for his own good. But people can change. What they can't do, though, is grow back missing body parts." She returned to kneading the dough, avoiding eye contact with Elisabeth. "Yes, I did get excited about the prospect of you finding a husband so soon. But then I realized that being married to him would mean more work for you."

Elisabeth's throat tensed. What business was it of Maria's when she was going after a man who put himself before his family? "I want a good man," Elisabeth said. "Someone who will treat me well. If that means more work for me, then so be it." She switched places with Rosina since Rosina's hands were neither big nor strong enough to truly knead the dough.

"Stefan's really nice and can be really funny," Rosina said. "And the end of his short arm is hard."

Both Anna and Maria looked questioningly at Rosina, as if to ask what her last observation about Stefan had to do with his suitability as a husband. The comment embarrassed Elisabeth, though, and she asked Rosina to not say such things about people.

Maria took a deep breath and looked at Elisabeth directly in the eyes. "You won't notice it at first, but after one or two children, you'll see how much more work it is for all of you." Elisabeth kneaded faster. "I don't doubt that he'll treat you well," Maria continued. "But if another man came along who was also really nice and helpful but had two hands, would you prefer to marry him instead?"

Elisabeth stopped. She wanted to say something mean

to Maria for asking such a question. Jesus implored His followers to accept all people: the poor, the sick, and even the lepers. But as she and Maria continued staring at each other, an uncomfortable truth arose in Elisabeth. The more she tried to push it down, the stronger it pushed back.

She would marry the man with two hands.

AUNT ANNE STOOD OVER THE SINK, TRYING TO SCRAPE OFF the last remnants of dough stuck to her hands.

"I had no idea it would be this hard," she said, sighing. "That dough was so sticky, and getting it off the dough hook..." She held up her hands, showing all the dough still glued to them.

All three kids were white with flour.

"We should've put on aprons," Aunt Anne said, returning her hands to the running water. "I'm so used to not wearing one that it didn't occur to me to put one on this time."

"Omama always wore an apron," Opa said. "So did your mother. They didn't get dirty like all of you."

Aunt Anne grabbed a plastic scouring pad and rubbed it on her hands. "I don't usually get dirty, either, but that's because I usually know what I'm doing. But, Tata, don't get up. The floor's covered in flour. We need to vacuum and wash it first so no one slips."

Her hands finally clean, Aunt Anne said triumphantly, "But at least we have two loaves of bread rising now and three batches of cookies ready to eat!"

Sophie and Dean snorted, and Juliana laughed quietly. The two loaves of bread looked more like small lumps of playdough, now hiding under a wet tea towel that had been spread over the bread pans. They couldn't be called bricks yet—they still had to go into the oven—so there was a chance they could become real bread. A small chance.

"Mom," Dean said, "we baked a better loaf back in grade three when we did the pioneer unit in class."

The girls chuckled at Dean's comment, but Aunt Anne raised her chin defiantly.

"They still have to rise. They're partially sourdough, so apparently they'll take some time. But you'll see—they'll be magnificent." She pointed a finger at her children and niece. "Complain any more—" She popped a freshly baked chocolate chip cookie into her mouth—"and you won't be allowed to have any of these," she said with a full mouth.

Aunt Anne had barely finished speaking when Dean swiped a cookie out from under her nose. Sophie burst out laughing, and Juliana had to join in. Even Opa chuckled along. Aunt Anne was a maven in the kitchen— Juliana had seen her successfully cook up scrumptious meals, with Aunt Anne cooking on all the burners and the oven at the same time as she assembled a gourmet salad. The cookies would obviously taste incredible. That made it all the funnier that Aunt Anne couldn't bake bread.

"You'd think with everything you learn in school they'd teach you how to bake bread," Opa said, a smile still on his face.

"Baking? In school?" Juliana asked. "Not in Calgary."

"Not here either," Dean said. "Our grade three teacher's husband was a baker, so he showed us. Otherwise, you have to take hospitality courses in high school for that."

"Your *omama*," Opa continued, "when she was younger, she would bake bread with her mother and sisters in this big..." His hands outlined a large rectangle. "I don't know what it's called. It was made from wood and they could bake lots of loaves at once. And I'm certain they didn't look like all of you when they were done!"

The kids laughed again.

"Fine, laugh all you want," Aunt Anne said. "But you all get to help me clean. Step outside and dust yourselves off while I get the vacuum." They quickly did as she said while she disappeared, but when they returned before Aunt Anne, Dean passed the plate of cookies around. By the time Aunt Anne returned with her clothes changed and carrying the vacuum, everyone—even Opa—had an innocent expression on their faces.

"Oh, I know that look!" Aunt Anne said. "I don't have to look at the plate to know you've *all* stolen a cookie. Even you, Juliana! I thought I finally had an ally here!"

Another fit of laughter overcame them.

Mom's missing out on all of this, Juliana thought.

Aunt Anne gave Dean the vacuum and left again. Dean clicked on the vacuum, and its loud motor filled the kitchen as he whisked the vacuum back and forth in no particular pattern. Aunt Anne returned with a pail and mop as Dean finished. She passed them to Sophie. "Start by Opa's feet," she said.

She handed a dishtowel to Juliana. "You can dry the dishes."

Opa pulled over a newspaper that was lying on the table and read while everyone else cleaned. Once everyone was done, Aunt Anne handed each kid a dishtowel to dry the floor right away.

As they dragged the dishtowels across the floor, Opa said, "Mammi baked bread every week for the rest of her life. Even when she could've bought it at the store."

Juliana lifted the wet dishtowel from the loaf pans and peeked at the bread. It looked a little bigger, but at that rate of growth it would take half the day before each loaf was the size of a real one. If baking bread took that long and only produced such slow results, she would be more than happy to buy what she needed at the grocery store.

Aunt Anne poured glasses of milk and pushed the plate of cookies to the middle of the table where everyone could reach. Dean headed for the basement with a handful of cookies to catch up on sports while Aunt Anne, Juliana, and Sophie joined Opa at the table.

"What was Omama's name?" Juliana asked. "I don't think anyone's ever told me."

An awkward silence followed as Opa stared at Juliana. "Elisabeth," he said. "Hasn't your mother told you?"

CHAPTER NINE

The lid was now on the trough so the dough could rise, and Elisabeth already had tea steeping in a pot.

"Thank you again for your help, Maria," Elisabeth said. "I'll do the rest this evening with my sisters. Can I offer you some tea and something to eat?"

Without waiting for an answer, Elisabeth brought a pot of chamomile tea and some bread, butter, and cheese to the kitchen table and invited her sisters to take theirs into the front room.

"That way we can talk privately," she whispered with a wry smile to Maria.

"I must admit," Maria said as she pushed her teacup toward Elisabeth, "it would be nice to have sisters to gossip with. Joschi—probably like Luki—would just run around and bother everyone if Tata didn't force him to help out."

Elisabeth poured herself some tea and nodded in agreement. Then she returned to the subject that weighed on her mind. "I understand what you mean about Stefan," she said. "But you don't know him like I do. He's kind, cares for everyone, and stands up for his friends. When I look at my aunts and uncles, I'm almost embarrassed to be related to them. I don't want that with my husband."

Maria took a sip of her tea. "But most don't see your aunts and uncles the way you do. Yes, your Peter-Bátschi and Sophie-Néni are...quarrelsome but they contribute to the church and take care of your grandmother. And your aunt and uncle on your father's side fulfill their duties, too. That's what's important."

Elisabeth buttered a slice of bread. "That's what Mammi said, too."

"Then you see? Sometimes it's not enough that a man is kind." Maria pulled the butter toward her and picked up the knife. She spread butter on her bread in slow, even strokes. "Family must always come first. It doesn't matter what has happened in someone's life." Her gaze met Elisabeth's. "You're right: Stefan is a very kind, honourable man. But he can't support a family. Who will plough your fields? Surely you don't think you're strong enough to do that."

"I'm sure we'd find—"

Maria didn't let Elisabeth finish her sentence. "And

what about Georg? Stefan is friends with him—and you know what I think of your cousin. The war is over and we live in peace again. There are many fine young men who are fifteen, sixteen, and seventeen years old who will not have fought in the war. You may have to wait a little longer to marry—it usually makes sense to wait until they've completed their military service—but then your *tata* will be home."

"Maria." Elisabeth's voice was becoming tense. "If I wait for a sixteen-year-old man, I'll have to wait at least four or five years! I'll be the oldest *großmädchen* sitting at the front of the church! I already turn fifteen this summer."

Maria reached over and placed her hand on Elisabeth's arm. "Then wait for those who are serving now to return. You need to think about your future. Where will your family be in twenty-five years? Will your oldest son be completing his military service? If so, you'll need a strong, capable husband to take over his chores while your other children grow up."

Elisabeth slid the plate of cheese to Maria, and Maria helped herself. Elisabeth then placed a few slices on her plate and bit into one.

"I'll trust in God," Elisabeth said as she chewed. "He will watch out for me."

"But God also wants us to act to help Him," Maria countered. "And remember that Stefan has been to war. I hear he has nightmares like the others. Can you imagine waking up in the middle of the night because your husband is screaming in his sleep? He'll wake up each baby. You'll never get any sleep. Hagel Konrad didn't fight in that war. That's another reason why I think he'll make a good husband for me."

As painful as Maria's comments were to Elisabeth, she remembered what Eva had once said about her worries: would her baby have the same fits as Georg? Where would Georg sleep so he didn't wake the baby at night when his nightmares overwhelmed him?

Did Elisabeth want to have those worries, too?

"I know of his nightmares," Elisabeth replied. "But I didn't think about how bad they might be. He doesn't collapse like Georg does and he says it's because he spent those two years in captivity."

"It's because he's a real man," Maria stated. "Georg isn't."

Elisabeth bristled. She had witnessed Georg's fits on two occasions in public and abhorred watching other men taunt him that he wasn't a real man.

Maria inched forward in her chair and took both of Elisabeth's hands in hers. "Lissika, I'm your best friend. I'm not saying any of this to hurt you. You can't ignore how hard things are now with your father gone. You have the biggest heart of anyone I know, but you need to remember that your marriage can help elevate your family. Stefan is a wonderful man. But marrying him would not change your future very much. He may be a man, but he doesn't look like one and can never fully act like one."

Stefan had been so helpful to Elisabeth's family that she hadn't considered the consequences to her family if she married him. Was Maria right? What if Tata didn't come back with the money he wanted to earn? Then it would be up to Elisabeth to marry well—if a richer family would have her—and that left her with few options.

"I really thought he would be good for you," Maria continued. "That's why I gave you that comb, and yes, I was teasing you Sunday morning, because I know you like each other. But I realized last night that marrying him might not help your family as much as you marrying someone else could."

Elisabeth sighed. Maria was right. Marriage wasn't only about her wishes; it was about her family's needs, too.

THE FOLLOWING MORNING, ELISABETH AND ROSINA WALKED to the store after Anna and Luki had left for school.

"Why are clouds white?" Rosina asked.

Elisabeth looked up at the sky. "I guess because God made them that way."

"But why?"

"Maybe because He wanted them to be pretty." Elisabeth hoped that would satisfy Rosina's curiosity. Unfortunately, it didn't.

"So He made the gray ones gray so they would be ugly?"

Elisabeth rolled her eyes, but her six-year-old sister was thankfully too short to notice. "Oh, Rosina, I don't know."

Elisabeth felt like she didn't know anything these days. *I spent two years studying for Sunday and I passed, but I feel like I know even less now.* Maria was right: a life with Stefan would mean more work. His arm would never grow back, of course, and given that Georg's nightmares weren't ending, Stefan's likely wouldn't either. *But he's so kind and helpful. Shouldn't those be the first qualities of a good husband?* But then again, his parents had no land outside the village, just their property and home and possibly a small plot in the vineyards—Elisabeth wasn't sure. With her family having only one son—so far, anyway—all of Tata's property would go to Luki and his future wife. Elisabeth would be stepping down in wealth if she married Stefan, not up.

"Lissika!" Rosina tugged at Elisabeth's skirt.

"What!" Elisabeth shot back.

"It's rude not to say hello!"

Elisabeth's attention returned to the real world where Maria, along with Little Sophie and her younger sister, Annika, were catching up behind them. Annika—a nickname for Anna, like Lissika was for Elisabeth—was the same age as Rosina. Little Sophie and Annika were running, holding their skirts up far too high, in what looked more like a race than an eagerness to see Elisabeth and Rosina. Maria was running too, but in a more ladylike manner, lifting her skirt only slightly and taking smaller steps. This meant she was far behind the others.

"I won!" Little Sophie cried out to her sister when they reached Elisabeth and Rosina.

Annika scowled. "You cheated!"

Now Little Sophie looked indignant. "How could I have cheated?"

"You ran faster!"

Little Sophie crossed her arms in a huff. But before she could continue the argument, Elisabeth interrupted.

"Hello, Little Sophie. What brings you and Annika out today?"

Little Sophie turned around to face Elisabeth, and Elisabeth had to lock her lips shut. Little Sophie's hair had been brushed back into an attempted braid but chunks of it already hung around her face, and a white kerchief hung around her neck like a napkin on an old person. Little Sophie tucked her hair behind her ears and retied her kerchief, with some hair still hanging around her face.

Annika piped up. "Mammi wants us to buy sugar."

"It sounds like she's going to bake," Elisabeth said, trying to find something positive to say about her aunt. "And how is Peter-Bátschi?"

Little Sophie shrugged. "Tata left this morning. We think he's going to the Braun *salasch* but we're not sure."

By now, Maria had caught up to the others. She and Elisabeth exchanged kisses, and Elisabeth was grateful to not have to continue with the current topic of conversation. Truth be told, she wondered if her uncle was actually at the tavern that lay on the way to Omama's *salasch*.

Annika and Rosina walked ahead of the older girls, kicking stones. Elisabeth admonished her sister to stop. "This time, *you* will polish your shoes if they're all scuffed!" she shouted. Rosina either didn't hear her oldest sister or—more likely—ignored her. Little Sophie shouted the same words at Annika, who turned around and stuck her tongue out at her sister. Little Sophie returned the favour.

They are wild animals, Elisabeth thought, remembering what Maria had called them.

"Has Frau Schuhmacher started on those new shoes yet?" Maria asked Elisabeth.

"No," Elisabeth replied. "With preparing for Sunday, we never really talked about it, and Mammi's not one to waste words."

Maria's smile turned into a frown. "I was hoping she'd be as excited about it as I am."

Elisabeth laughed out loud. "Mammi? Excitement?"

Little Sophie added, "Lissa-Néni is as strict as Omama and smiles even less."

Elisabeth shot her cousin a look. "That's a rude thing to

say!" At least here she could stand up for Mammi. Yes, Mammi was mean, but she was also working hard to support her family. Something her brother and sister-in-law did not do.

A defiant gleam in her eye, Little Sophie replied, "But it's true, and didn't we learn to always speak the truth?"

Little Sophie's reasoning puzzled Elisabeth. They did learn to always speak the truth. In fact, last week, when she was trying to figure out who in her family had stolen Maria's prized possession—a fashion magazine from America—Elisabeth had continually reminded her siblings of the importance of honesty. But it was also mean to say something like that about Elisabeth's mother.

"What shoes?" Little Sophie asked, not pushing the insult any further.

Maria jumped in, her excitement returning as soon as the question was asked. "My *oma*'s cousin sent me a fashion magazine from America, and they have the most elegant shoes."

Little Sophie's eyes grew wide.

Elisabeth continued the story. "Maria pleaded with Mammi to make her a pair of shoes like the ones in the magazine. Something different." She wanted to add that Georg intended to buy a pair for Eva, too, but Elisabeth suspected now would not be a good time to mention her cousin from the other side of the family. Little Sophie and Annika's father already mocked Georg whenever the chance arose, and Elisabeth was certain his children would do the same.

"I want a pair!" Little Sophie said. "Then all the boys will want to dance with me first!"

Elisabeth and Maria exchanged secret looks: how was Little Sophie's behaviour not an embarrassment to her family? At the same time, that was the third person...no...fourth...no...Elisabeth had already lost track of how many older girls and women liked the idea of decorated shoes. Once Mammi began making more modern shoes, the Schuhmachers would earn more money. *If I'm to be honest with myself*, she thought, *that might bring Tata home sooner.*

Her spirits high with the idea, Elisabeth silently forgave Little Sophie for her comments about Mammi and decided to do her best to enjoy the conversation, as idle as it was.

Elisabeth faintly heard the *clip-clop* of a horse farther behind her and didn't pay much attention to it until a man called her name. She, Maria, and Little Sophie gasped in shock when they turned.

Approaching them was Georg and his horse. However, instead of riding his horse, Georg was leading it, with Anna sitting sideways *in* the saddle. No woman—or girl—should ever sit on an animal! Men rarely did it themselves—most Semlakers she knew of, at least the Germans, didn't even own a saddle—and instead drove wagons. She had accepted that Georg liked to ride on the horse, but letting her sister ride on a horse challenged Elisabeth's desire to accept Georg's odd behaviours.

She walked up to them. "Georg," she began, not able to take her eyes off her sister.

He quietly held up his hand. "I'm sorry for this," he said. "But I found Anna sitting on the side of the road, crying. She couldn't walk and it wouldn't have been comfortable for her had I carried her all that way. Asking her to hop home when I had my horse also seemed cruel."

Anna's face was a little white, likely from fear but perhaps also from pain. Her left ankle was wrapped in a bandage.

"I've already taken her to the doctor," Georg said. "He said she needs to sit with her leg up for the next few days."

Elisabeth stroked Anna's leg. "What happened?"

Anna's mouth quivered as she tightened her lips.

"Shh, it's all right, Anni," Elisabeth said. "You can tell me when we're home."

Elisabeth called to Rosina, who was still kicking stones with Annika. Rosina and Annika turned and a moment later, Annika gasped and pointed at Georg, ran to her sister, and hid in her skirt while Rosina stayed where she was, her eyes fixed on the horse.

"Rosina!" Elisabeth called again, ignoring Annika's reaction to Georg. "Come! We have to go home!"

"I'll get her," Georg offered and handed Elisabeth the reins. But he only had to take two steps toward Rosina before she darted past everyone, made a bend around the horse by several metres, and rushed home. Elisabeth returned the reins to Georg and the two—with Anna on the horse—followed.

ELISABETH OPENED THE FRONT GATE AND GEORG LED THE horse through to the poultry yard so Anna wouldn't have to hop very far. But just when Elisabeth thought the day couldn't get any worse, Mammi came out of her workshop and saw her second oldest daughter perched on a horse.

Mammi's face turned red in an instant. "Georg!" she yelled. "What are you doing? Girls *do not* sit on horses!" Mammi kept yelling as Georg instructed Anna to place her hands on his shoulders while he lifted her off the saddle.

How does Mammi not frighten him like she does us? Elisabeth thought, as Mammi kept shouting.

"Rosina," Elisabeth said to her youngest sibling, "let Anna lean on your shoulder and help her inside." Elisabeth pushed Rosina toward Anna and opened the house door for them.

Rosina continued staring at Mammi, who was still shouting at Georg.

"Now everyone has seen my daughter on a horse!" Mammi continued.

Georg still showed no reaction.

Anna hopped toward Mammi. Her courage surprised Elisabeth. "Two boys from school teased me and began chasing me. They said I have no father. One of them shoved me and I fell behind a tree, and it really hurt! Luki had already run away to school." She burst into tears. "The boys called me a Gypsy!"

Elisabeth's heart broke. How could anyone be so cruel? Anna was at the top of Herr Blum's school, one of two schoolhouses run by the church. This one had grades three to six. So far as Elisabeth knew, Anna was usually quiet at school and generally well-behaved. Elisabeth could tell by the expression on Mammi's face that even she was hurt by the story. But a moment later, Mammi's lips returned to their usual thin line.

"Luki will be punished for leaving her like that," she declared.

"With all due respect, Lissa-Néni," Georg said, "Luki is only eight. The boys who did this to Anna would have been worse with him."

Mammi eyed Georg suspiciously. "You would know a thing or two about that, wouldn't you?"

"Which is why I'm saying it now."

As a boy, Georg had endlessly teased and ridiculed others in the school and village. Elisabeth remembered when she was Luki's age how she would try to hide from Georg—just like her siblings often did now—because Georg would tug at her braids. Even though Mammi was five years older than Georg, she hadn't been safe from his torments either. Once Georg began helping his father in the blacksmith workshop, he had grown in strength and had become one of the biggest young men in the village. He picked fights in the tavern and always won. His pride even led him to pick fights with lame Samuel. It looked like nothing would stop him from tormenting and belittling others—until he was conscripted to fight in the war.

"Anna has already seen the doctor," Georg continued. "She must keep her foot up for several days and not walk on it. She should see him again after Easter."

Mammi grumbled to herself. Elisabeth was ready to yell back at her for being so ungrateful. "I guess I owe you money for that," Mammi said.

Georg shook his head. "The second visit has also been paid for."

"I'm going to lose my place at the front of the classroom," Anna lamented.

Elisabeth stroked Anna's hair. "I'll teach you while you're home. Then you won't fall behind. When Herr Blum sees that you're still so very smart, he'll have to place you back at the front." Anna didn't appear too happy with that idea. Elisabeth sighed. Why was Anna so angry with her all the time?

Georg doffed his cap, placed one foot in a stirrup, hoisted himself up, and swung his other leg around. Mammi grunted and turned away, but Rosina stared in awe, her mouth still gaping once he sat atop the large animal.

"I believe we still have crutches from Samuel when he was young," he said. "I need to head out to the *salasch* immediately—we're continuing planting, including on your father's land—but I'll bring them by tomorrow if Mammi allows me to."

Georg and Samuel had offered to help Elisabeth's family with their land: with Tata gone and Mammi in the workshop, it was too much for them to take care of by themselves. *Another reason why Tata shouldn't have left*, Elisabeth thought.

As Georg turned the horse around, Elisabeth called out: "Wait! Don't leave yet!"

She rushed back to the kitchen, where she had ten loaves of bread ready to go. She packed two into a linen bag and hurried back outside.

"For you and Eva, and please give one to Samuel and Deaf Lissi."

Georg peeked inside the bag. "This isn't necessary," he said. "You have a lot to take care of."

"We helped," Anna added, pointing to herself and Rosina. "And Maria did too."

"It's not much," Elisabeth said, "but I wanted to say thank you. You've been so kind to us."

"Yes, thank you!" Anna added.

Georg nodded. "You're welcome."

Anna nudged Rosina to walk up to Georg.

"He's on a horse!" Rosina shouted back but Anna pushed her forward anyway. Rosina stumbled toward Elisabeth and grabbed onto her skirt. Sticking her head out from behind her oldest sister, Rosina squeaked out, "Thank you."

Georg smiled and nodded again. He wrapped the bag's handles around the horn on his saddle, kicked the horse to walk, and returned to the road.

CHAPTER TEN

nger welled up in Juliana. Why would Mom not tell her something so beautiful?

"But Mammi wrote her name with an *s*," Opa continued. "Your parents wrote your second name like they do in English, with a *z*." Opa shook his head. "How could Katy not tell you? We came to Canada for a better life. We didn't come here so our grandchildren wouldn't learn anything about their culture and their family."

Another awkward silence fell over the kitchen. Sophie stared at her lap. *She probably feels more trapped in this conversation than I do*, Juliana thought. But then her thoughts returned to Mom. What did Mom have against her family? And why wouldn't Dad tell Juliana? Or did Mom tell Dad what Juliana's middle name would be and that was that? *I wouldn't put it past her to tell him what to think,* she thought. *She does it with Opa and me, why not Dad?* Omama sounded like she was a wonderful person. Why would Mom want to keep this all a secret?

"Tata, that's enough," Aunt Anne said, pushing the plate of cookies even closer to him. "Now she knows. Leave the rest to Katy."

She pointed to the cookies, but Opa instead briskly folded the newspaper up and left to go to the washroom.

"I'm sorry," Aunt Anne said to Juliana, who grabbed another cookie. "Where Opa comes from is really important to him. He doesn't always understand what it means when we say 'times have changed.' But your middle name is your mom's story to tell, not his."

"But why is it so hard for her to tell me about it?" Juliana said. "And it sounds like Omama was really nice. The bits and pieces Opa's told me about her...in all honesty, Aunt Anne, it's helped me get through things here a little. Actually, more than just a little." Juliana took a bite of her cookie.

Aunt Anne sat down next to Juliana. "I was named after Omama's sister, Anna, but they wanted it to sound Canadian, hence Anne. When your mom was born, Tata and Modr decided to give her a name that was even more Canadian. They kept the K in Katherine to keep something German in her name, but otherwise, her name was new in the family. But when Peter was born, they fell right back into their traditions and named him after Tata. The whole son-pride thing."

Juliana had already guessed about who her aunt and uncle had been named after, but she couldn't figure out Mom. Now she knew why.

"But your mom opted for Katy: in her mind, that was more Canadian than Katherine. If we called her Katherine, she threw a fit. We just didn't want to deal with her tantrums, especially because we had three-year-old Peter's tantrums to deal with, too."

Juliana finished her cookie while Aunt Anne continued.

"The only child Phillip and I named after anyone was Sophie. Tata often talked about a cousin Sophie who was absolutely wild. With the way Sophie kicked inside me all the time, the name definitely fit."

Sophie blushed. "I like it."

"Good, because you're stuck with it," Aunt Anne said playfully. Sophie smiled as though she was grateful for finally getting a moment to breathe in what had begun as an uncomfortable conversation.

"But why wouldn't Mom tell me this? I mean, unless Omama did something absolutely horrible, I don't get why—"

Aunt Anne cut Juliana off. "You'll have to ask her. I'm sure she'll be angry when she finds out Opa told you. He shouldn't have said anything."

That didn't seem fair to Juliana. What was so wrong

with knowing that her middle name came from her great-grandmother?

The front door opened and closed.

"Hello?" Aunt Anne called through the house, but no one answered. She called again, but there was no reply. It took all three of them another split second to guess what had happened and they all rushed to the foyer.

Aunt Anne whipped open the door and saw Opa standing on the icy sidewalk in his stocking feet.

"Tata, come back inside!" she called.

"I have to go home," he said. "The news is on."

"You need your boots and jacket! Come back inside. You can watch here."

Opa shook his head. "Dean's watching sports. I don't like sports."

"It's too cold to walk outside in your socks. Besides, you can use the TV in the family room if you want to. Please, come back inside."

Opa glanced down at his feet and then at a small group of adults walking toward him on the sidewalk. Even the top of his head turned red. Juliana looked away when he came back inside the house.

Aunt Anne brought him back into the kitchen, asked him to sit down, and gave him a cookie, which he accepted. She ran up the stairs and returned with a pair of Uncle Phillip's socks and a towel. She helped Opa dry his feet and change his socks. Opa didn't look at anyone the whole time.

"But I want to watch in my bedroom," Opa said.

Aunt Anne rubbed Opa's shoulder. "Enjoy a few cookies, and then we'll get you home, okay?"

Opa nodded and bit into another cookie.

Aunt Anne took the cordless phone off the receiver and walked into the foyer. She kept her voice low.

"Katy? Good. You're home...Can you come by and pick up Tata?...He just stepped outside to go home and didn't have his boots on...But I don't want her to be responsible for him, even if it's only for three minutes...okay...in five." She hung up. Juliana heard her aunt let out a deep sigh but she had put on a happy face by the time she returned to the kitchen.

Five minutes later, when Aunt Anne opened the door for Mom, Juliana caught an exchange of looks between the two sisters, as though each one was annoyed with the other. She understood why Aunt Anne was annoyed with Mom. But what did Aunt Anne do to annoy Mom?

"Tata, give me your coat," Mom said, her voice impatient, once they were home again.

As Opa clumsily slipped his arms out of his coat, he tried to mumble an apology. "We were having such a lovely time. I'm really sorry, Ka—"

"It's fine." Mom took his coat to the hallway closet while Juliana stood in the doorway watching.

Opa tried to make eye contact with Mom. "Katy, please, I'm really—"

"I said it's fine. You wanted to watch the news." Mom glanced at the clock on the microwave. "It starts in two minutes."

Opa wanted Mom to hear his apology. So why wasn't she listening?

His shoulders slouched, Opa headed past Juliana and climbed down the stairs to his room.

Didn't Mom and Dad always tell Juliana to be nice to others? How many times over the years had they told her to not interrupt? Mom was treating him like a child.

"Why didn't you let him finish?" she asked Mom. "Aunt Anne did."

Mom whipped her head around and glared at her daughter. "Excuse me?"

"He was so embarrassed. He wanted to apologize, but you wouldn't even let him finish. Aunt Anne lets him talk. You just keep interrupting him."

Mom crossed her arms. "Thank you. I can tell what my father wanted to say."

"Then why—?"

Mom drew her lips into a thin line. "It's none of your business." She stormed off to her bedroom.

Great, Juliana thought. *Now that's two of us who are really angry.* Juliana wanted to ask about her middle name, but so much anger flowed through her that she needed to release it. Dancing would help. She took one step toward the basement door and stopped. Opa was downstairs, which meant he might come and watch her practise when she really wanted to be alone. *Or at least with a friend*, she thought.

She changed course and went to her bedroom and opened her laptop. Rachel was the only person who would understand right now.

Rachel's face came onto the screen, a smile on her face. "Two times in one week. I must be popular!"

Juliana smiled back. "We don't talk much, so I figured I'd see what you're up to." *What a lie*, she thought. But dumping on Rachel right away would've been rude.

"Cool! I'm not busy, and Miss Kasia cancelled dance tonight. We got walloped with snow."

"You, too? But it must be a big storm if classes in Calgary are cancelled. In Kitchener, if a few flakes fall, the whole city shuts down."

Rachel laughed and Juliana forced a laugh to join in.

"So, what's up? I can tell you're trying to look happy, but really, Jules, it's not working."

"I'm that bad at it, eh?"

"You wear your emotions on your sleeve. Even a bulky parka wouldn't be able to hide them."

Juliana told Rachel what had happened. "Then after Mom was so rude to Opa, I got angry at her, and now I don't think she wants to talk to me. But why was she like that to Opa? And why has she never told me about my middle name? I don't get it."

Rachel grimaced. "Man, that's tough. And right now, you want to dance, don't you? You're jittering. Shaking your leg again?"

Juliana parked her elbow on her leg and leaned her chin on her hand. "Was I wrong to get angry at her?"

Rachel bobbed her head side to side, suggesting that Juliana had overreacted a bit. "When we talked yesterday, you mentioned that you know this is tough on your mom."

Juliana began braiding her hair. Some part of her had to move. "Yeah, but she wanted to come here. Shouldn't she be happy to see him and be nice to him? She wouldn't even let him apologize to her."

Rachel didn't say anything for a minute, and Juliana worried she shouldn't have brought up her mother. After all, Rachel had just lost her mom not even two months before.

Rachel looked at her lap as she spoke. "I've never told anyone this, including that counsellor Dad's sending me to. But sometimes..." She hesitated.

"Rach, what is it? I know we don't talk as much as we used to, but you can still tell me anything."

Rachel nodded, her eyes still looking down. "Sometimes I do something exactly because Mom's not here anymore, something she would normally tell me not to do.

I mean, like, I should be cleaning my room because it's what Mom would want. But I don't want to clean it, and I like that no one's telling me to clean it anymore."

Juliana understood what Rachel was trying to say, that she felt guilty for not always wanting her mom to be around.

Rachel sniffled and wiped her nose. "The counsellor says that all feelings are normal when you lose a mom. But this one can't be. I mean, what kid doesn't want their mom back?"

Juliana didn't have an answer for that, so she stuck with the advice that Shawna at school had given her once: just listen. She didn't know how what Rachel was saying tied in with her anger at Mom, but Rachel clearly needed to talk to someone about this.

Rachel pulled a tissue out of a box and blew her nose. "I'm telling you this because I don't want to have feelings like that, but I do, and I can't help it. I wonder if your mom has feelings that she doesn't want, but she can't keep them inside."

Both girls sat silently for a minute or two. Juliana began to regret getting angry at Mom. She hadn't thought about that, obviously. Mom had wanted to move back to Kitchener... but maybe she had thought it would be different. But this was her father...but he wasn't the same as before...but...

"Listen, one thing I can tell you," Rachel said, "is to talk to your mom. She's around. So long as you have her, talk to her. Trust me: you'll regret it someday if you don't."

AFTER SUPPER, JULIANA CARRIED OMAMA'S BOOK INTO THE basement. It had been an uncomfortably silent meal and Juliana needed something to help her feel better afterwards. She wished Omama had written words next to her drawings so she could understand them. Which was why she was walking into the basement to see Opa: he could tell her what the drawings were about.

She knocked on his door and he invited her in.

"I wanted to ask you about Omama again," Juliana said as she held up the book.

"The news is all bad. Nothing new," he said as he turned off the television. He smiled. "I'm glad you like hearing about Mammi." He tapped on his bed and she sat down next to him.

"I looked at the next two pages," Juliana said as she turned on the voice recorder on her phone. By now Opa was used to her recording their talks. "But as usual, I don't understand what they're about." She opened the book to a drawing of the inside of a church, the pews decorated with flowers, and a picture at the front of the church of a man kneeling and looking up. "What's this one about?"

Opa gently lifted the book out of Juliana's hands and

put his reading glasses on. It only took him two seconds to recognize what his mother had drawn.

"This is Mammi's confirmation," he declared. "The students who were confirmed always decorated the church before the ceremony."

"What's confirmation?" Juliana asked.

Opa shook his head in dismay and Juliana immediately questioned her decision to come downstairs. "All three of my children are confirmed and none of my grandchildren are." He looked over his reading glasses at Juliana. "After two years of study, young people—they must be fourteen, your age—in the church are asked a lot of questions by the pastor. This happens on Palm Sunday. If they pass, they are adults in the church. It meant—at least back then—that they could go to dances and start finding a husband or wife."

Juliana's eyes almost popped out of her head. "They couldn't date until they did this?" How could a religious ceremony dictate if someone was an adult or not? She knew older teens who did not act like adults. How could one test suddenly make you act like one?

Still, it explained a bit why Opa thought Juliana was old enough to marry. And at least she had the answer to that first drawing, though it didn't excite her as much as she was hoping it would. *It was like Omama had an exam*, Juliana thought. She turned the page and showed Opa the next drawing she was curious about: a dinner table with several people on either side and an empty chair at the head of the table. "What does this mean?"

Opa again took the book into his hands but this time he needed a little longer before he spoke. "I think maybe this is the lunch after confirmation that day." He pointed at the empty chair. "That spot is for you." Juliana worried he was having another blip. As though he could read her thoughts, he smiled and said, "I am fine. But this is the family table, and Mammi's father is missing. Just like you've been missing at my table." Tears formed in his eyes and he dabbed them away. "I don't know why your mother took you away from us."

But she never took me away, Juliana thought. *I was born in Calgary.* She told her grandfather so.

"Family is supposed to stay together," Opa said. "Mammi told me to keep my family together. When your mother left, she took whatever family she was going to have with her."

That's stretching it a bit, Juliana thought. "But you came here," she replied. "And Omama's father left his family back then."

"Those are very different," Opa said matter-of-factly. "Your *oma* and I left Romania because of Ceaușescu."

"Bless you," Juliana said. But his confused look told her she'd given the wrong response—she hadn't meant it as a joke. "Sorry," she said. "I honestly thought you'd sneezed. What was that last word?"

"Ceaușescu. He was a Communist dictator." Now it was Juliana's turn to look confused, and Opa shook his head. "Another thing Katy never told you about?"

If she didn't get Opa back on topic, he would get sidetracked about this—whatever his name was. This dictator.

"You left because of him?"

Opa nodded. "We wanted freedom, something you young people don't appreciate." What was Opa talking about? Romania was in Europe. Wasn't Europe free? Opa interrupted her thoughts. "And Omama's father left to earn more money to support his family. He always planned to go home. But my Katy had no such plans. She just left her family behind." Tears returned to his eyes. "What did Irmgard and I do to drive her away like that?" He pulled a handkerchief from his pocket and blew his nose.

Juliana's skin crawled. This was not her responsibility. *Mom should be down here talking to him*, she thought. But Mom also seemed to be avoiding Juliana this evening. *Listening to a critique of my ballet performance would've been better than this*, she thought.

"I should probably do my homework," Juliana lied. The Alzheimer's counsellor had told her to make an appointment whenever she needed to talk. She would call in the morning, between periods at school.

CHAPTER ELEVEN

ark clouds were rolling in and Elisabeth could smell rain in the air. That meant there was little time to plant peas, so she set right to it. She was already behind with planting spring seeds for her first round of vegetables from the kitchen garden. *I don't even know what green foods we'll eat on Green Thursday,* she thought. *Pickles all day?* She was very behind in Easter preparations, but delaying the kitchen garden would have even worse consequences.

The stakes were already standing in their rows, so she simply had to push one dried pea after another into the ground.

Anna and Rosina were inside, Anna memorizing a passage from the Bible for school and Rosina hopefully dusting the front room. Although Anna didn't like taking orders from Elisabeth, she at least listened for now because she wanted to return to school and earn back her place at the front of the classroom. After asking Anna what she'd studied at school before her injury, Elisabeth had suggested what her sister could learn next. She also gave Luki clear instructions to write down what Anna's grade did in class and what the teacher told them to do for homework.

Elisabeth looked up when she heard the front gate open. Georg entered, two small crutches tucked under his arm. Elisabeth stood up and wiped her dirty hands on her apron.

"We finished planting your corn," he said. "We should be harvesting your winter wheat soon."

Elisabeth wanted to embrace him but she didn't think it would be proper. "Thank you. I can start helping you next week, as Mammi promised."

He nodded and then held out the crutches for Elisabeth to see. "May I show Anna how to use them?"

"Please do. I'll come in with you so I can see, too." It was really more an excuse than the truth: her siblings still sometimes ran from Georg, so she needed to make sure they would behave in his presence. "Besides, I should see if Rosina's cleaning like she's supposed to."

She closed up the jar of dried peas and placed her tools in their basket. "I just need to return these to the shed—it'll rain soon."

Normally Georg would only nod to acknowledge what she'd said. This time, however, he held eye contact with her, and an uncomfortable silence rose between them.

"Is everything all right?" Elisabeth finally asked.

Georg adjusted his hat before speaking. "I wanted to ask...how are you? My parents were unkind on Sunday, and I know how much you miss your father."

What should Elisabeth say? Not only did she not want to speak ill of his parents to him—that would be almost as disrespectful as a girl riding a horse—but women didn't talk with men about such topics.

"I don't mean to make you feel uncomfortable," Georg said, as though he knew what she was thinking. "But Eva told me what you told her on Sunday." At Elisabeth's alarmed look he continued, "I haven't told anyone else. She was worried about you and angry with my parents."

Elisabeth did want to talk about his parents with some-one, preferably a person who wouldn't spread her thoughts around the congregation. Georg was certainly someone Elisabeth could trust to not tell others, but could she speak openly when the topic of conversation was his parents? Would it be kind? At the same time, she had noticed Georg speaking up more this last little while. Was he beginning to feel more comfortable around her? If so, she was honoured by the growing trust he placed in her, but she wasn't sure she should share her real thoughts about his own parents.

"Lissika, the war..." Georg swallowed and Elisabeth

worried he might succumb to another nightmare. "The war...it was...I don't want to describe it. But I think you have an idea by now."

Elisabeth certainly did. She remembered Stefan once shouting at Peter-Bátschi about the nightmares—severed body parts flying through the air, close friends lying on the ground, bleeding to death and begging for help. She shuddered as she tried to shake those pictures out of her mind.

"When you fight out there, you..." He looked at her. He was obviously nervous about something. Was another fit coming on? What else made him nervous? Was it something she had said or done? "When you fight in a war, you start to believe that God doesn't exist." He stopped and took a deep breath, waiting for Elisabeth's reaction.

Elisabeth froze. How could someone not believe in God? She understood how much soldiers suffered. But to not believe in the existence of God? God always was and always would be. How could the world exist without Him? A shiver rippled through Elisabeth's body. Nothing about war sounded more horrific than that.

"I'm...I'm sorry you felt that way," she said, though her words felt like a poor acknowledgement of something so terrible.

"It's not something I say to many...I'm sure you understand why."

Elisabeth nodded. If others in their community knew

that Georg had stopped believing in God—even for a moment—they would torment him relentlessly.

Georg continued. "But when you wonder if God truly still exists, the first thing you do is to search for hope. It's not in the sky or in the land, because those two places—the most trusted places on earth to a farmer—have become the most dangerous. Most of us found hope in each other and in our dreams of returning home." Georg scratched the back of his neck and adjusted his hat again. "What I'm trying to say is that we men became used to sharing personal thoughts. It didn't matter if the man next to you was a Jew, a Gypsy, a Romanian forced to fight against his own people because he lived in Hungary, a Catholic...many of us didn't care about those things anymore."

Elisabeth remembered Stefan telling her the same thing once.

As a few raindrops began to fall, Elisabeth and Georg moved to stand under the overhang that ran along the side of the house. Elisabeth would have to put her tools away later.

Georg scratched his neck again.

He's really uncomfortable, Elisabeth thought.

"In Semlak, men talk with men, but not about these kinds of things, and women talk with women about...things that women talk about."

If Elisabeth wasn't mistaken, Georg's cheeks were turning red. Was he embarrassed to talk about this? But this must be important to him: he had never spoken to her this much before. From what Stefan had shared with her over the past couple of months, he and Georg talked a lot. And he obviously talked with Eva. But this was still too personal for Elisabeth. It wasn't that she didn't trust him. It was just that he was right: men and women *didn't* talk about these things with each other. That was just the way things were.

"I'm sorry," he said. "I truly don't want to make you uncomfortable. But you've seen my worst fears, and I've told you one of my terrible secrets. I know you won't pass it on to anyone."

Elisabeth immediately shook her head to confirm what he had said. But if not believing in the existence of God was one terrible secret, what were the others?

Georg continued. "You're young, and you have a great deal of responsibility on your shoulders because Lukas-Bátschi isn't here right now. What I'm trying to say is that... if you need any help, and especially if you're angry with my parents, please know you can talk to me. I no longer care for some of our rules." A small smile lit up his face. "That took a long time to say."

Elisabeth returned his smile. "I think you've said more to me just now than you have in the past year."

Georg shrugged. "Sometimes speaking is more important than listening to fears."

The rain began to pour down as Elisabeth and Georg went inside.

Rosina immediately ran to her sister, apparently not noticing Georg standing behind Elisabeth. "Anna said I'm being lazy! But she's still sitting at the table staring at a book!"

"I'm memorizing something Lissika gave me to do and you're fooling around with the toy basket!" Anna shouted from the front room.

"So it looks nice for Jesus!" Rosina shouted at her sister. To Elisabeth, she said, "Then she touches her ankle and stops staring at the book!"

"Because it still hurts!"

Georg coughed quietly. Both girls stopped and Rosina ran into the front room and pressed herself against Anna, who was sitting in a chair with her ankle resting on another chair. Anna smiled, which showed Elisabeth that at least one of her siblings was becoming more comfortable around Georg.

Georg hung his hat on the back of a kitchen chair and then held out the crutches for Anna. Her eyes lit up like candle flames.

"I adjusted them to your height," he said. "Would you like to—?"

"Yes!" Anna exclaimed. She winced in pain as she pushed herself up by bracing herself against the table while trying to keep her foot from touching the floor. Georg placed each crutch underneath her arms and explained how she should support herself on them.

Anna set the crutches slightly ahead of her and then hopped forward. She repeated the movements several times. Elisabeth noticed with dismay the light dents the crutches left on the mud-and-chaff floors. *That'll mean extra scrubbing on Saturday*, she thought.

Anna beamed at Georg. "Thank you! Now I can move around again!"

Georg nodded. "Start slowly—Samuel complained it hurt a lot under his arms when he first got them. And the doctor said to keep your foot up for a few days more."

Anna nodded as she moved around the front room, giggling at her newfound freedom, but Elisabeth had a feeling her sister was too excited to listen to him.

"After Easter Monday," Georg said, "I can take Anna and Luki to school in the wagon on my way to Samuel's on the mornings I go. Stefan said he can pick them both up on the mornings I have to stay in town." He smiled at Anna. "That way, you can get back to the front of the classroom quickly."

Anna grinned from ear to ear.

BEFORE THE SCHUHMACHERS SAT DOWN FOR LUNCH, Elisabeth and Anna told Mammi what had happened.

Unlike her daughters, Mammi did not smile. She sighed. "Then we must send Konrad and Margarethe a thank you."

"What?" Elisabeth asked. "Georg was the one who brought the crutches over and showed Anna how to use them." She had come to the end of her rope with Mammi's unwillingness to thank her nephew. "Doesn't he deserve something?"

Mammi's eyes glowed with anger. "You told me last night that you already gave him a loaf of bread. That's enough."

"But he brought them—"

Mammi interrupted. "And whose crutches were these?"

"Samuel's!"

"Did Samuel pay for them?" Mammi didn't wait for an answer. "No! Konrad and Margarethe did. You do not know *at all* what they went through when Samuel was sick. I wouldn't wish it on my worst enemy."

"But Georg still—"

Mammi wouldn't let Elisabeth finish. "Samuel's polio is *never* a topic one talks about with his parents. *Never!* That they allowed his crutches to leave their house and to be used by someone else is nothing short of a miracle."

"But they're cruel to Georg!"

"And they should be! You keep talking about doing God's will, Elisabeth Schuhmacher, and that includes sending a thank you to Konrad and Margarethe. You will cook them a gulasch and walk it over to them by four o'clock, before Margarethe and Eva begin preparing for their supper."

"But—"

Mammi held her hand out, ready to slap Elisabeth. "Enough!" She lowered her hand. "You are now an adult. Act like one and do your duty. Whether I like it or not, they are helping us while Tata is gone. You gave Georg your bread and did not think to send something for his parents? Maybe think back to what you studied, Elisabeth, and you tell me if your actions were just."

Elisabeth's anger choked her so that not a single word could pass her lips. Mammi was reprimanding her about not being fair? About not saying thank you to everyone who helped? *When she begins treating Georg with more kindness,* Elisabeth thought, *then I'll accept what she says about kindness.*

"Listen to me and do as I say," Mammi said. "You still live in my house, and as long as I am alive, I am your mother. You know what the fourth commandment says, and you will obey me."

Without another word, she sat down at the table, and everyone knew to follow her lead. As usual, no one was allowed to speak during the meal, but Elisabeth's mind was bursting with her true opinions about Mammi's decision.

And this time, she did not ask Jesus for forgiveness.

ELISABETH STARED AT THE HOT POT OF GULASCH SIMMERING on the stove.

"Before you accuse me of being unkind to Georg again," Mammi said, "remember that he allowed my brother to be killed in the war."

"He didn't—!"

"Enough, Elisabeth," Mammi said. "The three of you, go."

Why won't she listen to me? Elisabeth screamed inside her head. *Andreas-Bátschi and Georg were separated by their commanding officer. Georg had no choice but to leave him!*

Mammi handed Rosina a cloth bag with one of the remaining loaves of bread Elisabeth had baked two days before.

Elisabeth's anger had simmered all afternoon. That Mammi had insisted that the three girls go seemed dishonest. *She's making us do her work*, she thought. Elisabeth wasn't going to make it easy for Mammi. "Shouldn't you come, too? After all, they're helping your daughter."

Mammi placed her hands on her hips. "And how do you expect the shoes to be done in time for Easter?"

"This will only take—"

"Which would be time wasted not making shoes. Now go before I have you washing and ironing all your Sunday clothing again."

Using potholders, Elisabeth picked up the pot of

gulasch. Luki gleefully smiled at Elisabeth as he opened the door for her. "I get to help Mammi with her shoes."

If my hands were free, I'd throw that loaf of bread at him, Elisabeth thought as her anger rose yet again.

Rosina and Anna followed behind Elisabeth, Anna swinging carefully on her crutches. Elisabeth prayed for more patience, a gift God did not seem fit to bestow upon her.

None of the Ten Commandments says thou shalt earn money, Elisabeth thought. *Mammi just needed an excuse to avoid coming. They're not nice people, so why do we have to give them this while Mammi gets to stay home? It's not fair.*

"Did Samuel have these crutches when he was a boy?" Rosina asked, interrupting Elisabeth's thoughts.

"I believe he was Anna's age when he became very ill with polio."

"I was scared when Luki was sick."

"We all were," Elisabeth replied. She remembered the week Luki had come down with the Spanish flu. Although he had lived—and the three sisters had gotten it afterwards, though thankfully not as severely—other families had lost children to the same flu. *I guess Konrad-Bátschi and Margarethe-Néni would have been very frightened when Samuel was sick,* she thought. *What did they feel when Georg was at war?* Elisabeth realized that if her aunt and uncle were worried about one son, they must have been worried about the other, especially if the one away at war was the oldest. *And then he came back so changed, almost like his mind was ill instead of his body.* Was that possible? But Semlak had no doctor for the head, just the body. *I guess it doesn't matter,* she thought. *When someone is ill, their family worries.*

They came up to Konrad-Bátschi's home and could hear the *tink-tink* sound of two hammers on metal coming from Konrad-Bátschi's blacksmithing workshop. That meant that Georg and his father were not in the house, and that Elisabeth would only need to speak with her aunt. She breathed a sigh of relief. Although she believed she was beginning to understand her aunt and uncle better, it didn't mean she liked them more.

Elisabeth asked Anna to unlock the gates—she didn't want to dirty the pot by setting it on the ground, and Rosina was too short to reach the lock. After they passed through the main gate and the one to the poultry yard, all three sisters stood at the house door. Elisabeth told Rosina to knock.

Eva opened the door and clapped her hands in joy. "What are you all doing here?" she asked as her mother-in-law came up behind her, wiping her hands on her apron. "Please, come in."

As Elisabeth and her sisters entered, she caught a look of sadness fleetingly pass over her aunt's face when she saw Anna. Mammi was right, in a way: Margarethe-Néni was still sad about Samuel's illness, even though it had been a long time ago.

Once greetings were done, Elisabeth handed the pot of gulasch to her aunt.

"Thank you so much for your help," she said.

"Especially for the crutches," Anna added.

Margarethe-Néni took the pot out of Elisabeth's hands and Elisabeth shook out her sore arms while her aunt carried the pot to the table. Rosina passed the bread to Eva, who removed it from the bag and returned the bag to Rosina.

"This all smells very nice," Margarethe-Néni said without a hint of sarcasm in her voice. "I'm sure it will taste good." She looked at Anna again. "I understand my son placed you on a horse?" Anna nodded. "I'm sorry if he embarrassed you. It should not have happened."

Anna whispered, "My ankle hurt a lot and it was the best he could do."

Margarethe-Néni's eyes darted between Anna's face and her son's crutches. "If he'd had his wagon, he would've been able to bring you home properly. But he insists on riding that horse instead."

A silence followed and Elisabeth decided it was best to say goodbye. But before she could, Margarethe-Néni spoke.

"Your father wrote us a letter recently. He asked us again to help you."

Elisabeth clasped her hands behind her back and prepared for more criticism.

"That's why I allowed Georg to lend you Samuel's

crutches," Margarethe-Néni said. "And even if your father were here, this is something we still would have done."

"Thank you," Elisabeth said, and her sisters echoed her words. "We're very grateful." She felt an urge inside her to tell her aunt and uncle that she agreed with them, that she, too, wanted Tata home, but memories of their treatment of Georg stopped her from saying anything.

"Is there anything else?" Margarethe-Néni asked, now sounding more like her usual self.

"Thank you again," Elisabeth said, guiding her sisters out the door.

CHAPTER TWELVE

*J*uliana had just gotten home from the studio that night when Rachel called her on Skype.

"Hey!" Juliana said, so happy to talk with and see Rachel for the third day in a row. Although it wasn't the same as seeing her every day at school and at dance, it was better than the once a week or so they'd been talking since Rachel's mom passed away.

"Hey, I wanted to check in and see how you're doing. You were in such a dark place yesterday, I wanted to make sure you were okay."

Juliana took the elastic out of her hair and shook it out. "To be honest, I've tried not to think about it."

Rachel looked worried for a moment. "Have you talked to anyone about this?"

Juliana shook her head. "I tried to get another appointment with the counsellor we saw, but she doesn't have any openings until next week, and I can't figure out how I'm going to get to and from there without Mom and Dad knowing. Plus it'll cost ninety dollars. I don't have that kind of money."

Rachel looked concerned. "Jules, shouldn't you tell them? They'd want to know what's going on."

Juliana let out a snort. "My parents? You must be kidding. They seem to do everything possible to *not* be home. Especially Mom." She quickly plugged in her earbuds and microphone so she could talk more quietly without Mom hearing the conversation.

"I'm serious," Rachel said. "Didn't you tell me once that your mom and your dance teacher talked every week to make sure you're transitioning okay? And doesn't your dad call you on your walk home from school?"

"Well, yeah, but that's pretty much it. And Miss Denise said it was at the beginning. Afterwards, they were going to see if it was needed. No one's said anything, so I think they stopped."

"That still proves my point. They want to know what's going on with you. This is important. Parents can be annoying as anything, but, I mean, this is too big for you to go it alone."

Emotion welled up in Juliana and everything spilled out. "But Mom keeps going off to work and leaving me at home alone with Opa—and often it's okay, but sometimes it's a little scary. I thought at that last appointment that things were going to change, but they haven't. And then I got angry at her and all that, and she's hardly talked to me. She's my mom: it's her job to talk to me, isn't it? Dad said once that he was going to try and find a job that would let him stay in town, and that hasn't happened yet either. They're not making any changes, so I can't be that important to them."

Rachel leaned closer to her laptop. "It might look like that, but I still think you should tell them."

Juliana threw her hands up in the air. "Why? Mom doesn't even know what Opa's going through, and now he's talking *to me* about her instead of *to her*. I'm like the middle of a sandwich, Rach. Opa's sad that Mom moved to Calgary and he's talking to me about it. It's making me really uncomfortable. But when I tried to get Mom to listen to him, she got angry at me, not him. He was asking me all these questions, like why Mom took me away from him. How am I supposed to answer that?"

"Wait, what? You were born here."

Juliana sniffled and dabbed at her eyes again. "I'm sorry..." She blew her nose. "The counsellor told Mom that it's really important for the *whole* family to help look after him, especially if we're trying to keep him at home." She blew her nose again. "Mom wouldn't even spend time with him the other day—"

"I remember you saying that." Rachel paused while

Juliana got a fresh tissue. "You've had this problem before, haven't you?" Rachel continued. "When you were studying for your exams...and after that, you weren't happy with your marks and your dad made some kind of stupid comment? I mean, your dad's usually awesome, but...."

Juliana nodded. "Mom understood, but all Dad could say was that if he'd gotten the marks I had, he'd have been ecstatic. He might as well have said, 'My daughter's still a stranger to me.'" Dad's words crystal clear in her mind now, Juliana had to fight harder to stifle her tears—she didn't want to attract Mom's attention, and the doors and walls in the house were paper-thin.

"It sounds like when people tell me my mom's in here," Rachel said, pointing to her heart. "That's the stupidest thing ever. She's buried in the ground in a wooden box. What do people think they're doing by telling me that?"

Juliana blew her nose again and tried to regain her composure. "I'm so sorry. That's horrible. They don't get you either."

"It is what it is," Rachel said. "Have you tried dancing? It's helped me sometimes when Dad's not home."

"I can't dance right now because Opa comes and watches. And it's really sweet, but—"

"You sometimes need to be alone."

Juliana nodded.

"Jules, you can't keep all this from your parents."

"They know already! Well, about most of it."

"We've been friends forever, Jules," Rachel said. "If your marks aren't good, and you can't dance...you're going to go downhill fast." Rachel's eyes darted to the clock on her screen. "Listen, I'm giving you an ultimatum. First off, we're going to hang up soon, because you need your sleep. Second, I'm giving you until this time tomorrow night to talk to someone in your family. You seem to be getting along with your Aunt Anne. And what's your uncle's name?"

"Uncle Phillip? Or do you mean Uncle Peter?"

"The one who sounds bizarre but really nice. Not the boring one."

Juliana let out a little laugh. "That's Uncle Peter. But he's in France or somewhere."

"Then email him. I don't care how you get hold of these people. But if you don't *honestly* tell me tomorrow night that you've talked to one of them, I'm going to call them myself." Rachel looked straight into the camera on her laptop, giving Juliana the feeling that Rachel was looking her in the eyes. "Do you understand me, Juliana Roth?"

Juliana nodded.

"Okay, thanks, Dad," Juliana said on her cell phone as she walked home from school the next day.

"Sweetie, everything all right?"

"Yeah, why?"

"You sound kind of sad."

"I'm tired. Competition, dance, all that."

Dad sounded unsure, but he seemed to accept her excuse. "I'll be home in time to pick you up from dance tonight, okay? And your mom even has the afternoon and evening off."

"Sure, okay."

Juliana and Dad said goodbye to each other and Juliana slipped her phone back into her jacket pocket. Although Mom had seemed more relaxed this morning, Juliana hadn't wanted to blurt out to Dad what was happening between her and Mom and Opa. Judging by the fact that Dad didn't ask her more detailed questions, Juliana assumed Mom hadn't told him about what was going on either. That Mom had kept the origins of Juliana's middle name from her seemed almost unimportant now. She just wanted to stop being the monkey in the middle.

Dad has no clue what's going on at all, she thought. But the last thing she wanted to do was bring him up to date on the last few days while trying to avoid black ice on the sidewalks.

If she was going to keep her promise to Rachel, her parents weren't the family members to talk to. She emailed Uncle Peter a "hello, how are you?" email, and he responded, even asking if everything was all right. Had someone told him what was happening? Or was it too out of the ordinary that Juliana emailed him? Either way, she sent a generic "doing fine" response and thanked him again for his help with translating Omama's letter. She felt too uncomfortable dumping everything on him. *Besides, he's farther away than Dad is*, she thought.

That left Aunt Anne.

Juliana passed her own street and instead walked over a block to Aunt Anne's house. But when she got to the Morgans' front door, she began second-guessing herself. *I could just go home. I have until 9:30.* That was more than six hours away. *And if Mom and Dad are home, then maybe I can—*

Juliana jumped. Someone opened the front door.

"Oh, hey," said Dean. "Um, we're coming over to your place, you know."

"Could I talk to...um...your mom first? Aunt Anne? It'll just be for a sec." *Or half a year*, she thought.

"Mom!" Dean shouted through the house. "Juliana wants to talk to you!"

Juliana stepped inside.

"Oh, hey, Sophie," she said.

"Hey. Everything okay?" Sophie tucked her straight, blonde ponytail into her winter jacket and then zipped the jacket up all the way, including the collar.

"Um, yeah, I just wanted—"

"Hi, Juliana," Aunt Anne said as she came into the foyer. "Is everything okay?"

Now, Aunt Anne, Dean, and Sophie all stared at Juliana, who'd somehow imagined she'd be able to sneak in and out of their house undetected. Except by Aunt Anne, obviously.

"I, uh, I just wanted to ask you something."

"Sure. Shoot." Aunt Anne whipped on her jacket and slipped into her boots.

Juliana stared at the floor. "It's, actually, it's really nothing. I can talk to you about it later."

Aunt Anne seemed to notice Juliana for the first time. "You two go ahead," she said to Dean and Sophie. After they left, she closed the door. "Sorry, the day has been such a rush. Eye appointment for Sophie, then my own doctor's appointment, blood tests...and I'm sorry, I'm talking about myself." Aunt Anne took a breath and spoke again, her voice calmer now. "No one else is home."

Juliana stared at the wall.

"It's your mom, isn't it?"

Juliana nodded. Tears were threatening to fall, but she fought them back. She'd cried enough in the past day.

"What's going on?"

As though compensating for her pushing her tears back, words exploded out of Juliana's mouth in a volley of random thoughts and disjointed stories. Aunt Anne let her talk until she finished, without interrupting even once. It seemed like half an hour had passed before Juliana could stop, but a look at the hallway clock said it had only been five minutes.

"First off, come here," Aunt Anne said, her arms open wide. "I'm glad you came to talk to me."

Juliana let her aunt wrap her up in a hug. *Like the Rockies*, she thought. She could always count on Aunt Anne, it seemed. *More than I can count on my own parents.* Tears began to flow. They were not only tears of sadness but also of relief. Rachel had been right. She needed to talk with someone.

Once she and Aunt Anne let go, Aunt Anne asked, "Is there something I can do to help you?"

Juliana wiped her eyes and shrugged. Aunt Anne grabbed some tissues from the powder room and handed them to her niece. She placed her hands on Juliana's shoulders while Juliana blew her nose. "Listen, I will have to talk to your mom about this. You're her daughter."

Juliana pulled away, her eyes open wide. "Do you have to? She's going to be hurt that..." She didn't want to finish the sentence.

"That you came to talk to me first? I can handle your mom," Aunt Anne said. "I'll talk to her when the two of us have some time alone. I think this move has been harder on her than she anticipated."

Juliana had to agree with that much at least. "Just not today, okay? Please? She's already angry with me."

Aunt Anne looked Juliana in the eye for a moment and

then looked down at the floor. Juliana prayed Aunt Anne wouldn't tell Mom today. She wanted to make sure Mom was talking to her before Juliana divulged that she had spoken to Mom's sister first about all this.

Aunt Anne finally looked up. "All right. Not today. But I will tell her. If she knew something about any of my kids that was this important, I'd expect her to tell me."

Juliana nodded.

CHAPTER THIRTEEN

That evening, Elisabeth decided to write a letter to Tata: she missed him too much, and a letter was her only way of speaking with him.

Wednesday, March 31, 1920

Dear Tata,

Thank you very much for your letter. We received it on Friday. It was very helpful because Mammi accepted help from Georg and Samuel after she read it. They have offered to care for our land this year while you are away. Their friend Schäfer Stefan has offered to help, too. This week, Stefan built Mammi a small heating stove in the workshop so it's warmer for her.

But I'm writing not only to tell you what has happened, but also to say that I miss you very much. I really wish you had been at my confirmation. Your last letter was very nice, and I know you were thinking of me and praying for me on Sunday, but when I answered Pastor Fröhlich's questions, I didn't see you out there smiling at me. It made me sad.

We are taught to be honest, so I must tell you this: Sometimes I didn't hear Pastor Fröhlich, because I was thinking about you instead. I miss you a lot.

Did that sound like she was angry at Tata? She didn't want him to think that, even though that was how she was feeling. She quickly added,

Please don't misunderstand me! I know you are making a sacrifice so that we may have a better life. But that doesn't mean I miss you any less.

"But it also means I'm very angry with you. We don't need the money," she whispered as though Tata were there. She tried to ignore her anger. Maybe writing this letter wasn't a good idea. Drawing might help instead, like it had when she had drawn the lantern. She pushed the letter away and pulled her sketchbook toward her.

"But what would I draw this time?" she asked the blank piece of paper. "Me looking angry? Or me shouting at Tata? A pot of boiling water?" She deepened her voice, attempting to mimic her father's. "Lissika, I asked you to draw me whatever important events happened while I was gone. What is so important about a pot of boiling water?"

Then she switched to her own voice. "Because that's how angry I was the entire time you were away!" She clapped her hand over her mouth and looked through the kitchen to the front room. Her sisters looked up, but Luki continued playing with Tata's deck of cards. Elisabeth pushed her book away and brought the letter back in front of her.

"How do you deal with your family?" she whispered to Tata. "You make it sound so easy when you write in a letter that we should ask Konrad-Bátschi for help. It's horrible asking him for help." She tapped her pencil on the table. "You probably also know that we have no one we can really rely on right now and that your family is all we have." She raised her voice slightly. "Then why did you leave us?"

Elisabeth glanced up at Jesus hanging over the doorway. Jesus didn't answer her but she could speak her thoughts freely to Him and didn't need to worry about what she said.

"I once took comfort in knowing that Your Father was in heaven while You were on earth," she whispered to him. "It helped me after Tata left. But I don't have Your strength to accept that every day." Elisabeth remembered her conversation with Georg when he brought over the crutches. "But to not believe in You at all...I can't imagine a world that horrible. You will never make me live in such a world, I hope?"

Jesus stared at her, not giving her an answer.

Elisabeth read her letter again.

"What if he feels guilty because of what I've told him?" she asked Jesus. "I don't want him to..." *But maybe I do,* she thought, though she didn't dare say those words out loud, lest that make them more real.

She read the letter a third time. "We are taught to be honest..." There were several things she hadn't told Tata about yet: Mammi's baby, how mean Konrad-Bátschi and Margarethe-Néni were, that Stefan lifted her spirits almost as much as Maria did. *He would know all these things if he were here,* she reasoned with herself.

"If you're going to be gone," she said quietly, "then I should tell you *everything* that's happened while you've been away." Anger burned inside her now.

"What do You think?" she asked Jesus. "Your Father taught us to honour our parents, but each of my parents wants something different. I'm certain Tata would like to learn about our baby, but Mammi probably doesn't want me to tell him about it so he can focus on earning money instead of worrying about her and the baby." She reread the letter a fourth time. "Tata will not trust me if I write 'We are taught to be honest' and I lie to him."

That was a good enough reason to tell Tata about everything that was going on, wasn't it? Besides, Mammi never wrote Tata a letter—at least, Mammi had never given Elisabeth something to mail nor had she ever left the house Thursday mornings to mail something herself.

"If Mammi isn't going to tell him, then I will," she said. "After all, he is my father. He *should* want to know." She continued to write.

I don't know if I am supposed to tell you this, but I know that I must be honest with you.

What is making your absence so hard is that Mammi is expecting a baby. The midwife said several weeks ago that it would be three or four months before the baby is born. Mammi was getting very sick, so I had to call the midwife. That's why a heating stove is being built in your workshop. Mammi is doing much better now: she has been resting, but I had to find a way to convince her to listen.

Elisabeth let out her breath and reread the new paragraph. *Yes,* she thought as a new calm flowed through her. *No more secrets.* She recalled what secrets about family had done to Georg: they were part of the reason for his nightmares about his deceased wife and child.

The last thing I should tell you about is that Konrad-Bátschi

She hesitated. It was wrong to write something bad about his family to him, but writing about Mammi had brought Elisabeth relief. Would the same happen if she wrote the truth about Tata's brother, too? She could tell Tata about the lovely crucifix and lace she had received from her aunt and uncle instead. "No more secrets," she repeated. She kept writing:

is very mean. And so is Margarethe-Néni. They are so cruel to Georg, when he's in so much pain from the war. They say mean things to Mammi, and Mammi has to use all her strength to fight back. Why do we have to accept their help? Are we so alone in this congregation that no one else can help us?

Her anger overflowing, Elisabeth continued the letter:

And because you are away, Anna was teased by some boys on the way to school. They called her a Gypsy and said she lived in Harrisburg. You know that that's the nickname of the Gypsy settlement outside Semlak. They pushed her and she tripped, twisting her ankle. It hurt so much that Georg had to bring her on his horse back to us. That made Mammi really angry, and because I think Georg is a really nice person, she yelled at me, too, and she seems more angry all the time, especially at me. I know it's in part because of the baby

"Elisabeth!" Rosina called from the front room.

"What?" Elisabeth yelled back. Why did Rosina have to interrupt her now?

"I'm on the seventh row of my scarf!"

"Good for you," Elisabeth said half-heartedly. Quietly

to herself she added, "With any luck, it'll be done by the time you get confirmed."

Rosina had interrupted her thoughts, and Elisabeth forgot what she was going to write next so she put a period at the end of her last sentence, signed the letter, and put it in an envelope. She would mail it tomorrow.

Next, she pulled her sketchbook back in front of her. Her mind now surprisingly clear, she saw what she wanted to create on paper: her confirmation dinner, but with the chair at the head of the table empty. *That* she could explain to Tata.

THE POSTMAN FINISHED ANNOUNCING THE WEEK'S HEADLINES and handing out mail. As the crowd dispersed, a few remained behind to pass him their letters and packages. When it came for Elisabeth to hand him her letter, she hesitated.

"Don't you want to mail that?" Stefan asked. Stefan always came out every Thursday to see the postman. Georg usually did, too, but sometimes—like today—he had to help his father or brother instead.

"I'm not sure," she said.

"I must get on to the next village," the postman said.

"It's to your father," Stefan said. "That normally makes you happy, doesn't it?"

Something inside Elisabeth told her not to give the letter to the postman.

But Tata needs to know what's happening. It's his family, too. Maybe it will make him come home early.

"Miss?" the postman asked. "I must be going."

Her anger firing up again, Elisabeth thrust the letter at him. He tucked it into his bag, mounted his horse, and began trotting away to the next village on his route.

"Are you all right?" Stefan asked.

Elisabeth nodded. She didn't want to talk to him right now, especially because her discussion with Maria crept back into her head.

"You're much more quiet than usual," he said. "Is something wrong with the stove? I'll fix it—I want Frau Schuhmacher to be happy with it."

His concern made Elisabeth realize she was being foolish. *He's only asking how I am, not if I want to be his wife.*

"I'm sorry," she replied. "My mind is just elsewhere. But Mammi hasn't complained about the stove so that means she's happy with it." Normally she'd mean such a comment as a joke, but this time she meant it seriously. Little Sophie was right: Mammi was mean.

"Anything you'd like to talk about?"

She shook her head. "I'd just rather be alone right now."

Stefan's shoulders slouched. He removed his hat, placed it under his amputated arm, combed his hair back with his fingers, and then set his hat back on his head. "If you need anything, please ask," he said quietly.

Elisabeth didn't mean to hurt Stefan's feelings. She had to say something to cheer him up: sadness did not suit him, and none of this was his fault.

"Actually, I think we could use a little help with the stalls again. Would Saturday work? Or will you be busy with Easter preparations?"

Stefan's face brightened. "Modr and my sister will be looking after all of that. I can certainly come and help."

"And we still haven't had you over for dinner to thank you for your help with the stove."

His mood light again, Stefan replied, "I thought the bread was payment? It was delicious, and my parents shared the second loaf with visitors Wednesday evening."

How could Maria find fault with a man this kind?

"You've been a big help," Elisabeth said. "I'd like it very much if you stayed for supper on Saturday." She meant it. "We don't fast that day, just on Good Friday." Mammi had even told Elisabeth this morning they would not be fasting even though it was Green Thursday: they hadn't planted early spinach in time, and Mammi said she did not wish to eat pickles all day.

Of course, that's my fault, too, Elisabeth thought. But she didn't share that with Stefan.

Instead they arranged a time for Saturday before Stefan doffed his cap and they parted ways.

Elisabeth wished she could breathe in his happiness. Instead, a painful mixture of emotions filled her: anger at her mother's unfairness, butterflies in her stomach when she was near Stefan, fear from what Maria had told her about marrying Stefan, and frustration at Jesus for not offering a single word of help.

Why was *life* so complicated? She had learned all the rules, studied as hard as she could, had been confirmed, and yet nothing had taught her how to deal with her life. *And nothing has taught me how to deal with what I'm feeling,* she thought.

Not caring if she scuffed her boots, she kicked a stone all the way home.

If writing helped Elisabeth with her anger toward Tata, then cleaning helped with her anger toward the rest of her family. It was Saturday, the "big clean" of the week, when all the girls and women in a household scrubbed the house from top to bottom. *The Saturday before Easter should be called the "biggest clean,"* she thought dryly. But in truth, she didn't care, so long as she could keep moving.

Elisabeth had enough anger inside her to last at least a week between Rosina whining that she was knitting and not to be disturbed, Anna claiming that sitting and drying dishes hurt her ankle but playing at the table did not, and

Luki taking whatever opportunity he could to pull at his sisters' hair or tell Elisabeth what to clean next.

And tomorrow is Easter, she thought. *I can't be angry on the day of Jesus's resurrection.*

So she scrubbed harder and dusted faster than she ever had. Not even the tightest corners were hidden from her feather duster. Elisabeth had never cleaned their home so thoroughly before. She couldn't find a single dent in the floor from Anna's crutches by the time she was done.

"Anna, there are still water spots on these dishes," Elisabeth said as she saw the pile of dishes Anna had dried and stacked on the kitchen table. "Would you want to serve food to Jesus in those?"

Anna narrowed her eyes. "You can wash them again if you're so worried about them."

Elisabeth wanted to slap Anna with a dish towel, but that would simply bring her more trouble. Now that she was a *großmädchen*, Mammi would expect Elisabeth to behave like an adult. *But adults hit*, she thought, before admonishing herself for thinking that. Elisabeth refused to hit her siblings, despite the fact that Mammi did and that Omama had tried to make her do so once. She was certain Jesus did not approve of such actions.

"I'm going to take some food out to Luki and Stefan," Elisabeth told her sister. "You have a damp cloth there. Clean off the water spots. *Please.*"

Anna rolled her eyes at Elisabeth. *Why must she make*

my life so difficult? Elisabeth wondered as she picked up a plate filled with sliced sausage, whole pickles, buttered bread, and cheese to take outside. It was a warm spring day, and with Luki and Stefan cleaning up the animal stalls, it would be better if they ate outside and not in the kitchen. Plus it would keep Luki away from his sisters that much longer.

"Luki! Stefan!" Elisabeth called out.

"Still with the pigs!" Stefan replied.

"I'm helping, too!" Luki added.

"I've brought you some food. I'll leave it in the summer kitchen!"

"We'll be right out!" Stefan said.

Elisabeth was only too happy that Stefan—and not the Hagels—was helping her family this time. When Elisabeth had first noticed problems in the pigs' stalls, Omama and Mammi had called over the Hagels because they were carpenters, and because Konrad was seventeen and thus a potential husband for Elisabeth. It had gone so badly that Stefan and Georg had had to help corral the pigs after they'd escaped thanks to the Hagels' mistakes.

The summer kitchen was attached to the house on one side and the horse and cow stalls on the other. It was covered by a thatched roof and contained two benches, a long table, and an oven with openings at the top for a stove. It wouldn't be much longer before all cooking would move outside to this kitchen to keep the inside of the house cool in the summer. The Schuhmachers' summer kitchen was quite small, though, compared to the many others in their village, because Tata had taken a portion of it for his workshop.

We'll have to see who can take our cows out to pasture now that the weather has warmed up, Elisabeth thought. She would talk to Georg about that and see what he suggested. She didn't expect him to do it—he was already helping enough. But perhaps he—or Samuel—had an idea. *Might Stefan even do that? Or if I prepare myself properly, perhaps I could take the cows out at least once a week and take all my sewing with me. That would take care of at least one day.* She would need to think about it some more.

Mammi came out of her workshop, groaning quietly and rubbing her belly.

"I need fresh air," she said. "With the stove now, I can keep the door open, but it's not enough."

Elisabeth offered her something to eat and Mammi shook her head.

"Are you all right?" Elisabeth asked. "You look pale."

"I'm fine, Lissika. My health is no concern of yours."

Elisabeth sighed. Why did Mammi always say that? Obviously, Elisabeth had helped her already with her health. *And I have to look after the children more because of it. It is my concern.*

Mammi looked toward the pig stalls. The *tap-tap* sound of a hammer on a nail travelled across the yard.

"He is a good man," Mammi said. "It's too bad he doesn't look like one." With that, she returned to her workshop.

Elisabeth remembered what Maria had said about Stefan. *Maybe I should forget about him*, she thought. But she was lying to herself. His heart was good, and he treated her siblings like they were his own. Why did that not count for something?

CHAPTER FOURTEEN

*J*uliana and Sophie sat in the basement and paged through the first few drawings in Omama's book.

"How come you always look only at the beginning?" Sophie asked. "Aren't you curious about the rest?"

Mom had eyed Juliana suspiciously when Juliana entered the house with Aunt Anne. But Aunt Anne had covered for her and told her and Sophie to go down-stairs. Dean was sitting in the living room, talking with Opa.

"I was until Dad and I found this drawing..." Juliana paged ahead to the drawing of a man lying in his coffin. She ignored the drawings in between. She handed it to Sophie, who raised the book closer to her face to help her see the drawing better. "It's a man," Juliana explained. "Opa doesn't know who he is, but he's—this is kind of gross—he's dead in his coffin."

Sophie pushed the book away from her face. "For real?"

Juliana nodded.

Sophie wrinkled her nose and gave the book back to Juliana. "*Ew!*"

As morbid as the drawing was, Juliana was glad for the distraction. "I realized that Omama probably drew these in the order they happened, so I'd rather find out picture by picture. I don't want to know who that man is, so I'm trying not to jump ahead."

She turned back to the page of the table with the empty chair at the head. "I wonder what Omama would think of Opa now," Juliana said. "Do you think she hoped he would come to Canada?"

Sophie thought for a minute and shrugged. "Why would he even leave Europe to begin with? I'd love to go there someday."

"He said some name. Something about a dictator and... co...co...community? No, it was a different word."

"Communism?"

"Yeah, that's it. What is that?"

"No idea. Mom tried to explain it to me once, and she lost me fast."

"My mom can get like that, too."

"Why don't you search it online? Wikipedia should have something."

Juliana pulled out her phone and then changed her mind. When had she ever looked up anything about politics? It was all boring. "Maybe later. But I can tell you what Opa told me about the church drawing if you want?" She set her phone on the coffee table in front of them.

"Sure, why not?

"What are you girls up to?" Opa asked, surprising them. Juliana usually heard his footsteps coming. She hoped Opa wouldn't say anything about Mom. She was beginning to wonder if he hoped she'd tell Mom what he'd told her. "Dean wanted to watch his sports so he's in my bedroom right now, since your mothers are talking in the kitchen."

"I'm just telling Sophie more about Omama." *Keep him talking about Omama,* she thought.

Opa smiled. "That's nice to hear. Family was so important to her."

Juliana held her breath. That was his usual mantra for himself and his critique against Mom.

Opa sat down in the armchair just as a shout erupted from upstairs. "Say it, Katy! Tata has *Alzheimer's!* When will you finally accept that?"

Everyone in the rec room looked at each other.

Mom yelled back. "I know he does! You don't have to tell me the obvious! Why do you think I moved back here?"

"Then why do you keep running away? You came here to take care of him!"

"And we are!"

"Juliana is!"

"She spends time with him, Anne! That's hardly taking care of him!"

Tears rushed to Juliana's eyes and streamed down her cheeks. Of course she looked after him—she'd dealt with his outbursts and hallucinations, and had even cooked for him. How could Mom not recognize that?

But Mom didn't stop there. "Juliana spends time with your daughter, too!"

"What's that supposed to mean? That I'm not looking after her?"

"That's not what I said! You're twisting my words again!"

"That's what you're implying, *Katherine*! Sophie has a hard time in math, and Juliana's been a wonderful help!"

Sophie's eyes turned red. Both girls looked at Opa, who by now was gripping the arms of his chair, his face tight with anger.

"You—no, *your husband*—earns enough to get her a math tutor! So why my daughter?" Mom shouted.

"Has it ever occurred to you that maybe the two of them get along and like spending time with each other? Or are you too obtuse to see that, just like you can't see that your own teen daughter is looking after our father!"

"How can you say she's looking after him! I take him to his appointments, arrange counselling for Juliana *and* Sophie—"

"You do everything that doesn't involve *being* with him!"

"That's not true!"

Opa banged his fist on the chair. "No," he said, his jaw tight. "This isn't right. This is not why you're here, Yulika. You're here so we can finally be a family. You're not here so you can look after me."

Before either girl could say something, he jumped out of his chair and climbed up the stairs, holding on to the railing to keep himself steady.

Juliana and Sophie looked at each other, not sure what to expect next.

"The two of you *seid wie* children!" Opa shouted at Mom and Aune Anne, mixing his languages. "Your own *mädchen* are in the *keller* and they can hear everything *ihr sagt!*"

Silence followed.

Opa continued. "If this was *die heimat*, you would be kneeling in corn! As adults! I do not want to lose my memories, but I also did not want you to come home, Katherine Schuhmacher, *damit du und deine Schwester streitet!*" A bang on the wall startled the girls and then Opa shouted something short.

More silence, followed by Opa continuing to shout at his daughters, all in German now. Mom and Aunt Anne didn't respond, at least not that Juliana and Sophie could hear in the basement.

"Are you okay?" Sophie whispered to Juliana.

Juliana shook her head. "No. You?"

Sophie played with a thread on the couch. "Not really. I didn't want you to—"

Juliana grabbed Sophie's hand, drawing her cousin's attention. "I help you because I like hanging out with you. I'm not looking after you. If anything, you're the one looking after me. Got it?"

Sophie shook her head uncertainly.

"Listen," Juliana said, her voice firm. "You've made it a lot easier for me to get to know my family. You helped me when Kim died and I had no idea what to say to Rachel. You helped me search for Mom's photo—"

"I couldn't do much. You found it."

"Only because you showed me all the cool hiding places here. Sophie, you've got more spunk in you than anyone, probably just like that girl you were named after. I like being around you."

At that last comment, a small smile crept onto Sophie's face.

"This isn't your fault," Juliana said. "And it's not mine, either." Anger rose in her. "None of this is fair! What is it with these stupid adults? It's like you and I don't have a say in any of this!"

The shouting upstairs stopped. Juliana and Sophie heard the stairs creak with the sound of Opa's footsteps. He appeared in the doorway, his face sad now.

"I'm so sorry, Yulika," he said. "And also to you, Sophie. That is not how adults behave. You are my grandchildren. I hope you know how much I love you." He paused, and still no sound came from upstairs. "They love you, too. They just act like donkeys sometimes."

Opa's comment surprised the girls.

The stairs creaked again and soon Mom emerged in the doorway with Aunt Anne behind her, their heads bowed in shame.

"Juliana," Mom whispered. "I'm sorry."

Juliana didn't want to hear it. She jumped up from the couch, mumbled an apology to Opa and Sophie, and pushed by Mom. "Leave me alone," she said. "Just stop pretending like you care." From halfway up the stairs she shouted down, "And just so you know, I emailed Uncle Peter and talked to Aunt Anne first!"

Before Juliana turned around to go back up the stairs, she caught a glance of Mom's face with its mixture of hurt, confusion, and sadness. Juliana understood in that moment how much she had hurt Mom with her comment.

But why should I care? She doesn't.

She ran up the rest of the stairs and into her bedroom, slammed the door, dropped onto her bed, and bawled into her knees.

CHAPTER FIFTEEN

ontinuing with the big clean, Elisabeth climbed on top of a chair in the back room and dusted the top of the wardrobe that stored their Sunday clothing and shoes. She stepped down from the chair and dusted the front, carefully pushing the feather duster into the carved corners of the wooden doors. Next, she moved over to a set of drawers that kept the family's mittens, shawls, special handkerchiefs, and purses. Hanging above the drawers was a framed photograph: Mammi and Tata on their wedding day. Elisabeth knew that having a photograph taken back then was very expensive. This one had been a special gift from someone in Mammi's family, but Elisabeth didn't know who. Although the photograph had been hanging there for as long as Elisabeth could remember, only now did it awaken any emotions within her.

"I'm trying to accept that you had to leave," she said, looking at Tata's face in the picture. "But I still find it very hard. We celebrate Easter tomorrow, and you'll again be missing."

As tears formed in her eyes, she wiped them away. Mammi would be angry at her for crying. mocking her mother's tone, Elisabeth said, "We have to keep going."

Finished with the dusting, Elisabeth looked in on Rosina in the kitchen and was happy to see that her youngest sister was still washing potatoes. In the front room, Anna, her leg propped up on a chair, sat at the table surrounded by piles of laundry she had folded.

Luki burst into the kitchen from outside, holding a shoe. "Look! Mammi finished all her orders early today, so she tried something!"

He held in his hand a black satin slipper with simple floral embroidery on the toe. Like a normal women's dress shoe, this one had no heel or buckle but the toe was more pointed than usual. *It looks lovely,* Elisabeth thought, *but without the heel, it doesn't look as modern as I had hoped it would.*

"It's elegant," she said, which was the truth. Mammi's handiwork was always exquisite.

Luki shoved the shoe in Rosina's face, startling her. She dropped a potato on the floor and cried, "Now I'll have to wash it all over again!"

Luki stuck his tongue out at her.

"Can I see? Can I see?" Anna asked from her seat in the front room.

Luki rushed in and held it in front of her face. "But you can't touch it," he commanded. "Your hands have to be clean."

Anna snatched the shoe from her brother. "I'm folding clean laundry, you dumb donkey! Of course my hands are clean."

Luki pulled his hand back, ready to swing at her.

"Luki! Anna!" Elisabeth scolded. "We celebrate Easter tomorrow! Remember what Tata says: Jesus is always watching."

Luki dropped his hand but still stuck his tongue out at Anna, who tried to swipe him with her hand but couldn't reach him.

"Did you not hear what I just said?" Elisabeth shook her head at her siblings.

"Get Mammi a snack," Luki commanded.

"Pardon me?" Elisabeth asked.

Luki repeated his command louder.

"I can hear just fine," Elisabeth said. "But what word are you missing?"

"Mammi said her stomach is sore, so you have to get her a snack now. Bread with paprika."

Elisabeth wanted Luki to say "please," but the mention of Mammi's pains made that unimportant. As Elisabeth prepared Mammi some bread with paprika, she asked Luki more about Mammi's pains but he only shrugged.

Elisabeth hurried. *Is the baby all right?* she wondered. When she arrived in the workshop with the snack, Mammi seemed fine.

"The women had better buy these shoes," Mammi growled. "They take longer to make, so they'll be more expensive. And if they want heels, then they'll have to pay for my new lasts." She pointed to the wall of lasts—wooden forms of feet in different sizes that were used to make shoes. Mammi held up the second shoe and scrutinized it.

Suddenly without warning, she cried out, dropping the shoe on the table, wrapping her arms around her belly and doubling over in pain. Elisabeth's stomach flew into her throat and her heart beat faster than the hooves of a galloping horse.

"Come inside," Elisabeth said. "You can lie down on a bed there."

"No!" Mammi shouted as another shot of pain pierced her. When she could breathe easily again, she said more calmly, "The children are inside."

"I'll send them out to play."

Mammi glared at Elisabeth. "Our neighbours will see me. I'll deal with this here."

Elisabeth had had enough of Mammi's stubbornness. When she had been sick earlier in the winter due to the baby, Mammi had refused to ask the midwife for help. Even after the midwife had come at Elisabeth's insistence, Mammi had said that the visit had been a waste of money. But once Elisabeth had convinced Mammi to follow the midwife's instructions, Mammi's health had improved.

"The neighbours have already seen the midwife visit you. You don't need to keep this a secret but you do need to come inside."

Mammi gripped her stomach as pain overwhelmed her once more. "They talked about it at church for weeks because of you!" She took a few deep breaths as the pain appeared to subside. "I have to finish this shoe so I can show this new style to customers on Tuesday." She sat up straight and reached for her small hammer.

"Now you can walk," Elisabeth said. "Come inside. I can make you a tea..." What else could she offer Mammi? She knew very little about having babies. When Mammi had first been sick, Elisabeth read about pregnancy in Tata's encyclopedia, but once it started describing Mammi's shame area, Elisabeth had slammed the book shut. *Now I wish I had read all of it*, she thought. But it was too late. Mammi screamed and collapsed onto the floor. Elisabeth saw a stain of blood through the back of Mammi's dress.

"I'm getting help," Elisabeth said. She didn't wait for Mammi to respond but instead ran toward Konrad-Bátschi's and Margarethe-Néni's house, lifting her skirt to her knees to give her legs as much freedom as possible. Mammi's sisters lived farther away, Sophie-Néni couldn't look after her own family much less help her sister-in-law, and Omama had trouble walking. Margarethe-Néni was the only woman Elisabeth knew who could help immediately.

She banged on her aunt and uncle's door until someone opened it. It was Eva.

"Elisabeth? What's wrong?"

"Where's Margarethe-Néni? I need her!"

Margarethe-Néni hurried to the door before Eva called her, a look of concern on her face. Elisabeth asked that Eva leave the room: she didn't want to cause her worry about her own baby.

Elisabeth spoke in a low voice. "Mammi has very bad pains in her stomach and..." She couldn't speak the next words: doing so would make Elisabeth's fear real.

"Tell me everything," Margarethe-Néni said, "so I know what I need to bring along."

Elisabeth had no choice. She pushed the words out of her throat. "There was blood on the back of her dress."

Faster than a strike of lightning, Margarethe-Néni collected rags, old towels, and a tattered apron into a bag.

"Get the midwife," she commanded Elisabeth. "Where is your mother?"

"In the workshop."

Margarethe-Néni hurried out the door toward Elisabeth's home while Elisabeth ran to the midwife's house. There she banged on the door again and the midwife answered immediately. When Elisabeth told her what had happened, Frau Mólnar grabbed her bag and sprinted past Elisabeth to Elisabeth's home. Already tired from the run to Margarethe-Néni's and then to the midwife's, Elisabeth's legs burned, slowing her down.

By the time she arrived back at her own house, Elisabeth saw Mammi limping between Margarethe-Néni and the midwife, spikes of pain clearly still ravaging her body. Elisabeth hurried to open the house door so the three women could enter the house.

"Everybody out!" the midwife said, startling the children inside. They dropped what they were doing and stared. They had never seen Mammi so weak. "Now!" the midwife ordered.

Elisabeth passed Anna her crutches and grabbed a few of the children's toys. She shooed them out of the house, not knowing where they should go.

As the midwife and Margarethe-Néni carried Mammi to her bed, Margarethe-Néni said, "Go back to my house. I will come for you when I can."

Elisabeth thanked her as she exited the house and closed the door behind her. She saw small pools of blood on the ground between the house and the workshop. Bile darted up her throat but Elisabeth pushed it back down. *Not now,* she told her body.

"What's wrong with Mammi?" asked Luki. "Did you tell her you didn't like the new shoes?"

Elisabeth's anger and frustration burst out of her and she struck Luki's cheek. When he cried out in surprise, Elisabeth shouted, "You deserved it!" Anger flashed in her eyes as she stared down at her sisters. "You would've deserved it, too, if you had said anything. I have tried so hard to help everyone and when Mammi needs us to listen to her because she's in pain, the first thing I hear is that it's my fault."

"I'm telling her you hit me!" Luki screamed.

"I don't care!" Elisabeth replied. To her surprise, she realized she was telling the truth. Elisabeth was certain Mammi's baby was dying because of the blood on her dress and the ground. The encyclopedia had said this was called a miscarriage, and Elisabeth could do nothing about it. But nothing else mattered to her right now.

When they reached Konrad-Bátschi's and Margarethe-Néni's house, Eva immediately offered everyone freshly baked Easter cookies. It would've been polite to refuse the special sweets so they could be saved for tomorrow, but Elisabeth didn't have it in her to speak up.

"Coffee?" Eva offered.

Elisabeth shook her head. She had never tried coffee because her parents hadn't bought any since the war. The last thing she wanted right now was something new. Elisabeth buried her face in her hands and sobbed uncontrollably. Her siblings began to cry, too, even Luki.

"Water?" Eva asked. When no one answered, she filled

cups with water from the jug. Elisabeth tried to drink, but she could only muster a few sips.

Eva rushed out of the house and reappeared with Georg a few minutes later. The children were so upset that they didn't even notice him coming inside.

"I don't know what to do," Eva told her husband. "Something's very wrong with Lissa-Néni. Mammi's over there right now."

Elisabeth didn't want to say anything to Eva or in front of her siblings, but she had to do something and praying right now didn't feel like enough. *I'm sorry*, she said silently to Jesus. She handed her bag to Eva.

"For the children," she said between sobs. "I need fresh air." She hoped going outside would calm her down. The neighbours didn't matter either; whatever was happening with Mammi would be spread around the congregation by tomorrow morning.

Georg instructed Eva to stay with the younger siblings while he followed Elisabeth outside, bringing her cup of water with him.

CHAPTER SIXTEEN

*J*uliana swung her dance bag over her shoulder, kept her head low, and hurried out of the studio. Her one hour of tap tonight was barely enough to keep her from exploding. Now she had to get in the car with Dad, and she was almost as angry at him as she was with Mom.

Except that I've hardly talked to him for days, Juliana thought. *And why might that be? Oh, right. Because he's never home.*

Her parents hadn't been home at the end of Juliana's first exams in Ontario. They were hardly home to help her deal with the death of Rachel's mom, and they were certainly almost never home on Opa's bad days.

Juliana yanked open the car door, threw her bag on to the backseat, dropped into the passenger seat, slammed the door shut, and belted herself in. All without making eye contact with Dad.

"I hear things haven't been going very well again." Dad backed out of his parking spot.

Juliana said nothing. Why start now?

"Jules, I'd like to know what's going on. Mom told me about the argument and everything."

"Then there's nothing else to say," Juliana said as she looked out the window into the dark.

The streetlights flew by, each one replaced by the one following it. The car kept on driving, but the string of streetlights went on and on. *Just like every day passes by*, Juliana thought, *and my parents still act as though nothing has changed.*

"Jules, I feel like our relationship has improved over the past few months, and I'd like it to continue that way. I really want to hear your side of the story."

Sure, Dad would be home all of tomorrow, but on Saturday he had a short-haul drive to Ottawa and back, and then he'd be home on Sunday and Monday, only to get back into his truck on Tuesday to drive down to Atlanta, Georgia. What was the point? None of this could be solved during the few days Dad was home, and even though he often said she could call him anytime, that wasn't really true. Sometimes Dad was in heavy traffic, at the border, at an inspection station, or grabbing a nap.

Dad spoke again but this time his voice was tense. "I

know I'm not around often, but I've told you why I do what I do. My choices coming out of high school were the military or trucking. I didn't have the opportunities your mom had."

"All she does is manage a grocery store." The moment those words slipped out, Juliana regretted them. They were harsh, even for an argument with her parents.

"What's that supposed to mean? What's wrong with managing a grocery store?"

Juliana hadn't meant it to sound that way. She kept hearing about how getting a university degree was supposed to land you awesome jobs and awesome pay, and here was Mom with *two* degrees, working a job that didn't seem to pay as much as Juliana had once thought and that seemed to need Mom all the time. *But Dad won't understand that*, she thought. Juliana didn't want to talk about it any further. "Nothing."

They stopped at a red light. Dad turned to face her. "I'm trying to be as patient as I can be, but you're really pushing it. I really mean it when I say I want to hear from you what happened."

"You're gone most of the time anyways, so why does it matter?" Juliana kept staring out her window.

"What else am I supposed to do? Wash cars?"

"What's wrong with that?" She was pressing Dad's buttons, but he was doing the same to her. "If managing groceries is fine, then so is washing cars."

"It's minimum wage, that's what's wrong with it!"

"The light's green."

A car behind them honked and Dad stepped on the gas.

"Listen, I'm asking because I love you and I want to help. How can you not see that?"

Juliana's voice dripped with anger. "Maybe because you're not around to show me?"

Dad began shouting at her, but Juliana tuned him out. Seriously: what did it matter? Nothing was going to change, just like it hadn't the first time all of this came up.

THE SIDE DOOR TO THE HOUSE CRASHED OPEN AS JULIANA stormed through.

"You have no idea how good you have it!" Dad shouted behind her as he came in.

Juliana stopped in her tracks, turned around, and glared at her father. "Here's the idea I do have! I have friends whose parents are around. Shawna sees even more of her one parent than I see of both of mine put together!" She threw her bag into the kitchen.

"You were fine with our schedules in Calgary!"

"Because that was home and I could stay at Rachel's!"

Juliana kicked off her boots and they tumbled down the stairs into the basement.

"Pick those up before someone trips on them!"

"Mom's already up here and Opa's probably watching TV!" Juliana stomped past Mom to her room.

"Don't talk to your father like that!" Mom shouted down the hallway.

Juliana whipped her bedroom door back open, stuck her head out, and replied, "You mean like how you talk to yours?!"

"We're both adults!"

"Then act like it!" She slammed the door shut.

Through her walls, Juliana could hear the basement stairs creak: Opa was coming up. For a moment, she worried he might actually trip on her boots, but he made it to the kitchen without an incident.

"Please, stop," Opa said. "All of you." He raised his voice a little—but his tone was not angry—and called down the hallway to Juliana to come to the kitchen and to bring Omama's book. She reluctantly obeyed: she was arguing with her parents, not him, but she avoided eye contact with Mom and Dad when she came back into the kitchen.

"You're fighting more than Irmgard and I did when we first arrived in Canada." He reached his hand out for the book of drawings and opened it to a drawing of two men. It was a later one, one Juliana and Mom had seen before, a drawing of a skinny man with only one arm who had that arm around a bigger man.

Opa held the book up for everyone to see. "Katy, in all the years you lived at home, I never told you about this man—Georg. He couldn't look after his family, and by the time his last child was out of school, his family had fallen apart. Mammi and Eva, his wife, were best friends for many years, but Eva was always sad because she didn't know how to keep her family together. But Mammi—your *omama*—did."

Opa was trying to make a point, but his complaints about a man who probably had post-traumatic stress disorder only added to Juliana's anger.

But before she could say anything, Opa closed the book and looked directly at her. "I love you, Yulika, but sometimes you expect too much from your parents. They work very hard to give you a nice life. You should—"

Now I'm in trouble again, she thought. She wasn't going to back down now if Opa was going to side with her parents. "But they're hardly ever home," she said.

"And they haven't taught you to not interrupt," Opa said sternly.

Opa's pushback surprised Juliana. Was this another one of his blips? *I hate not knowing what's normal for him!*

"Tata, there's no reason to—" Mom began.

"And you've clearly forgotten, too."

What was going on here? Was Opa hallucinating that he was back home again? His arguing with Mom and Aunt Anne had made sense: they were his daughters. But now with Juliana and Dad in the room?

"All of you are talking about me," Opa said. "Now it's

my turn." He faced Mom and his voice softened. "Katy, I don't know what Modr and I did to push you away, but—and maybe you won't believe me—but I'm so happy you're home. My family is together again."

Mom opened her mouth to say something, but no words came out. Opa lovingly rubbed her shoulder.

"For the first few years you were gone, I said—do you remember?—I said, 'When you're home, we will—'"

Mom joined in. "—go to SportsWorld and play mini-golf and go down the big slide."

Opa sighed. "I'd forgotten that it's gone that day we drove by there with Yulika. You were right—I did know." He looked at Dad. "Paul, thank you for working so hard to take care of my daughter and granddaughter. Being away from family is really hard. I thank God every day that you agreed to move here."

Dad nodded and smiled, and Opa patted him on the arm.

Opa spoke to all of them now. "If this horrible thing that's happening to my brain is what brought you all back, then I should thank God for that, too. Mammi taught me that the most important thing a parent can do is to keep his family together." He looked at Mom, who already had tears in her eyes. "You know I only speak up when I really have to. It seems like I have to a lot these days, especially when everyone is angry at each other."

Mom began to sob, and Dad rubbed her back.

Juliana's anger flew out of her body like a flock of birds dispersed by a stone. But she still didn't like being home alone so often and she didn't like only seeing her parents in the car on the way to or from dance. Was now a good time to speak up or was it best to say nothing? She remembered how Opa had told her a few times that she often didn't say enough when something bothered her. Eventually, she would fill up with anger and her words would explode out of her. *And it happened again*, she realized. But Opa had also told her a few minutes before to not interrupt.

"I just...I don't know...I felt like I never fit in," Mom said between sniffles.

Juliana chose to wait, at least for a few more minutes.

Opa took Mom's hands in his. "You've always been a special girl. You have a special name."

Mom rubbed her nose on her sleeve and Dad handed her a tissue. "Annie was named after your aunt," Mom said, "and Peter after you, but I was named after no one. Peter spent all those summers with you in the factory, and Annie and Modr always cooked together for hours in the kitchen. And where did that leave me?"

Opa cocked his head to one side. "But you always wanted to dance?" He seemed genuinely confused, and Juliana didn't get the sense that it was a blip.

Mom shrugged. "I loved it, but I somehow felt different, I guess, from everyone else."

Opa and Mom hugged for so long Juliana feared they

would melt together. Was now a good time to speak up? *The worst that's going to happen is that they're going to yell at me, and they were already doing that*, she thought.

"Mom? Dad? I...can I say something?"

When everyone turned to face her, Juliana realized she'd rather be on stage with thousands of eyes staring at her than in this tiny kitchen with the three pairs of eyes that were staring at her right now. But she needed to say something. "It's just that I don't really like being left alone so much," she said. "I mean, I'm old enough to stay home alone, and I can cook for myself, but that doesn't mean I want to be left alone all the time."

Mom wiped her eyes and Dad ran his hand through his hair, but it was Opa who spoke.

"Yulika, it's hard to start a new job when you've been doing the same one for a long time. Life hasn't been very easy for you, but life was very hard for your *omama*. Very hard, especially much later, after she finished drawing in this book. But she pulled through. You're a Schuhmacher. You can be strong."

Mom spoke up. "Tata, she's only fourteen."

"Only, Katy? She's *already* fourteen. She's very responsible, and I can trust her to be honest. If she lived in Mammi's time, she would be ready for a husband."

Juliana's worries about Opa's mind returned but they were quickly erased as he continued.

"Things are different here," he admitted. "They tear

down buildings and put up new ones. Back at home, you only did that if a fire happened or when the Communists wanted to build something new. Yes, it is different here, but Juliana's still old enough to be a woman."

Opa's words surprised Juliana. She didn't consider herself a woman, not by a long shot. She would become a woman when...she didn't know when it happened. But not at fourteen. She couldn't even drive yet.

"Peter," Dad said, "your mother had almost no education. If I understand what Katy has told me about her and what Juliana has said, too, she finished in grade six and then took over her household. That's a lot of responsibility for someone so young, but that's all she had to worry about. Her future was laid out for her: she was going to marry and become a housewife. Done. Juliana's still in school. Her days are filled with learning. We hired cleaning help for your house because we're all too busy to do that ourselves. Yes, she's growing up, and faster than I'd like to admit, and she's shown a lot of strength already, but she's still not an adult yet."

Opa pulled out a chair at the kitchen table and sat down. "My legs are getting tired," he said. He winked at Juliana. "The Schuhmacher Shuffle can take its toll on an old man's body." Then his face became stern and he banged his finger on the table. Juliana jumped, but Mom didn't move. "And your arguing will take a toll on my family."

Wait...was Opa...no...was he? She waited to see what he would say next.

"If Juliana is expected to do all this learning and dancing and isn't old enough to look after a household, then she needs parents around to help her."

He laid a trap! she thought gleefully. Opa was definitely not having any blips. This was an *excellent* day for him!

"But you just said you know how hard it is to change careers," Dad protested.

"Paul, I grew up in a Communist dictatorship, changed *countries*, and had to learn a new *language*. And you've just said your daughter isn't old enough to look after a household." Opa tapped his head. "Some days, I'm still smart like a fox."

Juliana almost wanted to do a scorpion—a jump in jazz where her back leg bent up to touch her head and her front leg kicked out straight. But aside from the lack of space in the kitchen, Juliana's scorpions needed a good deal of work, so she imagined herself doing a perfect one at the studio instead.

Opa stood up and headed to the stairs. "My mind is going, and it's not fair to expect such a young woman to look after me. If you're going to live here to help me as I lose more and more of my memories, you must be here more often. I'm sorry you've had to change your lives for me, but, as I said, if my Alzheimer's has brought my family back together, then it's helped me do what Mammi always told me to do. I'm going to watch the news. The three of you must talk." Without waiting for anyone to respond, Opa returned to his bedroom.

No one said anything right away. Juliana could see that Opa's cunning reply had stung her parents, but in a good way. Mom and Dad glanced at each other and then at Juliana. In unison. *That's creepy*, Juliana thought.

Mom broke the silence. "I'm sorry," she said.

Dad started, "Just because we're your parents—"

"Doesn't mean you're perfect," Juliana finished. Her parents said that often. *Though sometimes not often enough*, she thought. "But I wish you'd see what's going on right in front of you."

For once, Mom and Dad didn't yell at her. In fact, they gave each other concerned looks.

"Your job is so close," Dad said to Mom. "You're always a walk or short drive away if there's an emergency. It doesn't make sense for you to find something else." Juliana's heart sank. Had no one heard a thing she and Opa had said? "Which leaves me, and the only way I'm going to be able to change careers is to probably go back to school part-time. And I don't know if I can do it."

Dad had said as much a month or two back, but nothing had ever come of it. Would this time be different?

Mom squeezed Dad's hand. "Lucky for you, two-thirds of your family are excellent students." She winked at Juliana, and Juliana didn't have the heart to say to her that her marks at school were slipping. *I'll tell them another day,* she thought. *Along with asking about my middle name.*

"Maybe it is time to at least *consider* it," he said. "But listen, Jules, this isn't something I can do overnight. It's going to take time."

Juliana's heart sank some more but Mom opened her arms to Juliana and Juliana accepted, hugging Mom back. Dad wrapped his arms around both of them.

"Try to think of it like this," Mom said gently. "This move has been really hard on you because you've had to deal with a lot of change: new school, new studio, new school system, new friends, maybe even new ways of talking to people. When an adult changes to a new career, all those things happen, too."

Juliana nodded. She had to admit that made sense.

"But," Dad said, getting himself a glass of juice. "I can see about talking to a career counsellor or someone like that. I have to start somewhere, right?"

Mom kissed him in agreement.

Juliana cringed—she didn't like it when her parents did that in front of her. But she nodded, also agreeing with Dad. It was a start. *I guess we've all had to make changes to come here,* she realized. *To help keep the family together.*

CHAPTER SEVENTEEN

"Is Lissa-Néni in pain?" Georg asked, closing the house door behind him.

Elisabeth nodded. "And she..." Would saying anything about blood cause Georg to have another fit? Could she even tell him what she believed was happening? What if it reminded him of his first wife and baby? They had died from a fever, but it was close enough, wasn't it? "She couldn't stand up," she said, which was the truth.

"You're afraid she'll lose the baby."

Elisabeth looked up at him. How did he know? She nodded, too tired and distressed to try to change the subject.

"It's easier this way, if it's God's plan to lose a child," he said. "Once a baby is born, it is suddenly a life you care for."

He paused, lost in thought. "It's much harder to say goodbye once you see that life."

Elisabeth dried her eyes with the back of her hand. "We don't have to talk about this," she said.

He waved her concerns away. "Yes, we do. You were too young when Anna's twin died during birth, but you know that your mother also lost one baby before you, and that I lost both my first wife and child."

Elisabeth nodded. Part of her wanted to end this discussion; it made her uncomfortable to be talking about such private matters with a man, even if he was family. Moreover, she didn't have enough strength inside of her to help him if his nightmares overcame him. But she needed to talk to someone about this. Maria had never experienced something this sad before, not to mention the fact that she would likely gossip about it to others. Moreover, Elisabeth wasn't close with family on Mammi's side, and any other friends she had would surely gossip, too.

And Tata's not here.

Elisabeth clapped her hand over her mouth. "The letter! I just wrote Tata that Mammi was expecting a baby! Now he's going to tell everyone—"

Georg shook his head. "Semlak is your father's *heimat*. He knows no one here discusses such news outside the family until the baby is born. But he will be sad when he finds out what's happened."

Elisabeth began to cry again. "I was angry at him, so I

told him to make him feel bad. I told myself it was to be honest with him, but that was a lie."

Georg gently lifted Elisabeth's cup of water to her lips. She took a few sips.

"I'll write to him," he said. "He's your father and will understand. You'll need to look after your mother in the coming days and weeks."

Elisabeth forced herself to breathe more slowly so she could speak. She had one important question to ask Georg about the babies Mammi had lost before, though she feared the answer.

"How was Mammi after Rosina died?" Because Anna's twin was named Rosina but didn't live, the next girl to be born received that name. It was tradition to make sure family members were continually honoured in later generations.

"Very angry," Georg replied. "She shouted every day at Lukas-Bátschi, and I'm sure you were very frightened of her when you were young."

A shiver travelled down Elisabeth's back. "I still am."

Georg shook his head. "I'm certain this would have happened earlier if you had not called Frau Mólnar when you did the first time. You have more courage than you realize."

Elisabeth appreciated Georg's compliment, but how did he know about that visit? It took Elisabeth only a moment to answer her own question: anyone who had seen Frau

Mólnar come to the Schuhmacher home would've said something. And if they hadn't, Frau Mólnar would've said something to someone, anyway. All that was needed was for Herr Meier—the church gossip—to hear about it, and he would have passed it around the church before the service even started.

"Are you coming, you lazy mule?!" Konrad-Bátschi shouted at his son from their workshop.

Georg sighed. "One moment," he said to Elisabeth.

As Georg spoke to his father, Eva came outside. She rubbed Elisabeth's back. "Would it help to talk to me? Woman to woman?"

Elisabeth took another sip of water. "I'm so grateful to have you and Georg right now."

Eva smiled. "Can I ask what's wrong? Is your mother sick? Injured? Will she at least be all right?" Eva's arms protected her growing belly. "I heard Margarethe-Néni say to call the midwife. She isn't...?"

Elisabeth nodded. "I think so."

She glanced over at Georg and Konrad-Bátschi. Her uncle was shouting in his son's face, but Georg wasn't even wincing.

"How does he take that?" Elisabeth asked Eva, trying to change the subject. "I would run away crying."

"Both Mammi and Tata are like that with him," Eva said. "My own parents yelled at me often the way all parents do, but it was nothing like what happens here. It terrifies me, even though they only shout like that at Georg, and sometimes at Samuel. But Georg says that if he has a kind side, then his parents must have one, too."

Elisabeth had to admit to herself that she had seen glimpses of that side of her uncle. However, as she and Eva watched Konrad-Bátschi yell at his son, pause while Georg replied, and then begin yelling again, Elisabeth realized they were truly only glimpses. *Did Tata see those, too?* she wondered. Why else would he tell Elisabeth to ask his brother for help when both Konrad-Bátschi and Margarethe-Néni had made it abundantly clear that they disliked helping his family?

Konrad-Bátschi threw his hands in the air, turned on his heel, and stormed back into the workshop. Georg returned to Elisabeth and Eva, and a moment later, all three could hear the clangs of Konrad-Bátschi's hammer on iron.

"I only told him that your mother is ill and needs Mammi's help right now," Georg said. "And that you need mine. I didn't say anything else."

Elisabeth drank more of her water. "Thank you, but it's just as well. Word will have spread by Easter service tomorrow morning." She already dreaded all the stares. *I'll be sitting in front of everyone*, she realized. Suddenly, she wished she hadn't passed her confirmation: then she could sit in the balcony with the children tomorrow where the adults couldn't see her.

Georg stared at the ground, Elisabeth played with a few strands of her hair, and Eva picked at a stain on her apron.

"Actually," Eva said, breaking the silence, "I came out to say that the children have calmed down. The toys you brought them helped. Anna and Luki got into a fight, but I offered them cookies to stop." She smiled at her own idea. "It worked."

Elisabeth finished her water. "Has Luki said anything about me hitting him?" she asked. Georg raised his eyebrows at Elisabeth and she looked down at the ground, ashamed. "I was so angry and frightened about Mammi," she explained, "and then he accused me of being selfish, and before I knew it, I'd hit him."

"There is far worse," Georg said, his voice calm. "He's a boy. I'm sure he's used to it."

"Maybe. But I didn't even care that I had done it. Not at the time." She felt sick now that she had hit her brother when she believed so strongly that Jesus did not want adults hitting children.

"What we feel inside can burst out of us," Georg said. "Sometimes it can't be helped."

That was the last thing Elisabeth wanted to hear. "I have to find an answer. Maybe not today, but very soon."

Eva smiled. "You can give them cookies instead. They stop fighting that way."

Elisabeth smiled, too, but shook her head. "They'll get fat if you give them too many."

Eva kissed Elisabeth on the cheek and squeezed her hand. "I should go back in to make sure they're all right. But we're family, Lissika. If you need help, you can come to us."

Elisabeth nodded and thanked Eva.

After Eva closed the door, Elisabeth slumped against the house's white wall. "Mammi has been so angry these last few months, Georg, that I don't know if I can handle any more of it. I can't strike my siblings again." She peered through the window into the kitchen and saw Luki playing with his dried cobs of corn and a rubber ball on the floor. "How can I be expected to raise them *and* deal with Mammi's anger?" She turned back around to face Georg.

"I understand how much this troubles you," he said. "But your parents know how to keep your family together. Lukas-Bátschi does it with his letters to you, and even to my parents. Lissa-Néni does it by working in your father's business and teaching you how to care for your siblings. Your children will learn the same from you, and your grandchildren from them, your great-grandchildren from them, and so on. You will make it through and you will keep your family together, though it won't be easy."

Georg's words sewed themselves into Elisabeth's heart.

CHAPTER EIGHTEEN

The week was finally over and Juliana had some time to hang out with Sophie. They entered the café in Belmont Village, a shopping strip that was a thirty-second walk from both of their homes. The café had a bit of a 1950s feel to it, with a pink, black, white, and chrome colour scheme. But the tables and chairs looked thoroughly modern with clean, simple lines. Orderly, just how Juliana liked things. *Not how my life has been recently, though*, she thought. They found a table by the window. The longtime owner of the café, Casimiro, an older man with a strip of white hair around the sides and back of his head, came up to take their order. Juliana could see his wife in the kitchen.

"Let me guess," he said in his Portuguese accent. "A tea for Miss Roth?"

To his and Sophie's surprise, Juliana shook her head. "I'll take a milkshake today, please," she declared.

"Not your usual?" he asked, confused by the unexpected change. "You always ask for tea or water."

"I'm in the mood for something different," she replied.

Sophie said, "Well, I just saw pigs fly."

Juliana playfully swatted at her cousin.

"And for you, Miss Morgan?" Casimiro often called the girls by their last names for fun. It made Juliana feel special and grown up at the same time.

Sophie said right away, "I'll take a root beer float, please."

Casimiro nodded approvingly. "Your mothers both loved root beer floats when they were your age."

"I've never had one," Juliana said. "What do they taste like?"

Sophie's eyes opened wide. "They are to die for!"

Juliana liked the idea of trying something that Mom and Aunt Anne both liked. Given all the recent fighting, it sounded kind of peaceful. But she had one question. "What did Uncle Peter always drink?"

Casimiro's aging face wrinkled like a raisin as he smiled. "Your favourite: peppermint tea."

"My preference for peppermint tea is genetic? From Uncle Peter? Oh, man." Juliana sarcastically clapped her hand over her eyes, only to uncover them a moment later as she laughed. "Now I have to try the beer thing," Juliana said.

"Root beer float," Sophie and Casimiro said together.

"Yeah, that."

After Casimiro left, Sophie placed her elbows on the table, folded her hands together, and rested her chin on top. "You look happier," she said.

Juliana leaned back in her chair. "I am and I'm not. I'm still kind of angry that it's taken me this long to meet all of you." She tucked her hair behind her ear. "But there was another big argument after dance the other night—I kind of started it, I guess. But Mom eventually told Opa that she felt left out because of her name. I'm sure there's more to it —adults are complicated. But I guess it's hard to stay somewhere when you feel left out."

Sophie sat up. "I guess that makes sense. That's what Mom was sort of saying when we were all baking, right?"

Juliana nodded.

Casimiro returned with their drinks. "Here you go, lovely ladies. Two root beer floats."

Juliana thought that Casimiro's use of "lovely ladies" was a bit creepy, but Mom said he'd always done that and that he didn't mean anything bad by it.

"Anything else I can get you?"

Both girls shook their heads. Sophie slipped the straw right into her mouth and started drinking.

Juliana did the same and a split second later pulled her

head back, almost spitting out her drink. "Oh my god, what is that?"

Sophie burst out laughing. Several other customers also turned to stare at Juliana. *This is not the kind of spotlight I like*, she thought.

Casimiro turned around, shocked. "You don't like it?" he asked. "I can get you something else. The Schuhmachers are some of my best customers."

Juliana waved her hand. "No, no, it's okay," she said. "I'm just not used to this, that's all."

Casimiro nodded in acknowledgement and left the two girls alone. Everyone else returned to their conversations.

Juliana leaned forward and whispered, "I have to drink *all* of this?"

A hint of mischief in her eyes, Sophie said, "Yup!"

Juliana sighed and this time took a slow sip. She cringed even at the tiny amount that had made it into her mouth. It had a dry, bitter...it tasted gross. There was no getting around that.

"If you let the ice cream melt a bit then the root beer isn't so strong," Sophie said.

Juliana accepted any excuse to delay taking a third sip and began stirring her drink with her straw.

"But to be honest, Juliana," Sophie said, "me and my siblings fight like that a lot. It's nothing really."

"Nothing?" Juliana looked at her drink. "That seemed really mean, the way Mom and Aunt Anne shouted at each other." She brought the drink up to her lips and shook her head. Not yet. She'd try again, but not yet.

"You'd probably say the same thing if you heard us fight," Sophie said. "I mean, just look at Rebecca."

Rebecca was the oldest Morgan child at age twenty-three. "Yeah, she's a piece of work," Juliana said. "What she said to you that one time about trying to make you ask for things and stuff. I had no idea sisters talked like that to each other." Juliana brought the drink up to her lips. "Nope, can't do it."

Sophie laughed as Juliana stared into her float. "You'll get used to it, don't worry. What I love about this is that it's sweet and kind of creamy and vanilla-y, but the spices in the root beer also tickle your tongue."

"Tickle your tongue?" Now it was Juliana's turn to snort.

Sophie playfully crossed her arms. "Then what would you call it?" And to tease her cousin more, Sophie looked directly at Juliana—though she was really looking through her—let out every last molecule of air in her lungs, and slurped up at least two inches of her drink.

"All right, fine," Juliana said. "I'll give it one more try." She sarcastically massaged her cheeks and stretched her mouth. Then she licked her lips, smacked them together a few times, and swallowed. "Here goes nothing!" She stuck the straw in her mouth and took the tiniest sip. "Ahh!!!" she said as though she were on some soft drink commercial. Sophie was beside herself with laughter, but to Juliana's surprise, now that the ice cream had mixed with the root bear, it tasted pretty...*I refuse to admit it*, she thought but she took another sip.

The words flew out. "I think I like it now."

Sophie stuck out her hand. Confused, Juliana took it and Sophie shook hands vigorously. "You've witnessed a Schuhmacher sibling fight, and now you like root beer floats. Welcome to the family!" Sophie raised her glass, which was more than half done. "Here's official recognition that within three months you have officially become a Schuhmacher of K-W."

They clinked glasses and Juliana grinned from ear to ear. Although she'd always think of herself as a Roth from Calgary, she liked also being a Schuhmacher from K-W because it meant that she could begin to feel at home.

"You know what?" she said after taking another sip of her float. "Opa said something yesterday about Omama always keeping family together. I guess he means that we help each other get through things."

Sophie drank half of her remaining drink before responding. "As much as I hate this," she pointed to her eyes, "my family—and that includes you—is helping me through it. And I think we've helped you, too? Like with moving, and Rachel's mom dying, and getting used to this wacky family."

"Oh my god, Sophie, you guys have been such a huge help! I can't thank you enough."

"Well, if you could somehow teach my mom to bake decent bread, I'd take that as a thank you."

Both girls laughed.

"Did the bread taste bad when it was done?" Juliana asked.

"Worse than that. The house smelled so awesome, and then the bread came out as hard as..." Sophie faked a drum roll on the table.

"Two bricks?" Juliana guessed.

"Bingo."

The girls drank their floats in silence for a minute, and Juliana enjoyed the sensation of the different flavours on her tongue. "Tickling" was indeed the right word for it.

"But you're right," Juliana said. "Whatever happens to us, we somehow seem to pull through. We can even laugh about bricks of bread."

Casimiro came by the table. "Well, Miss Morgan, I can see that you loved your root beer float as usual. And Miss Roth..." He gave an approving nod: her glass was only half full. "Looks like you've learned to like it."

Juliana nodded. "It grows on you."

"Excellent," he said. "Another generation of Schuhmachers loves our root beer floats. Can I take a picture for our Facebook page?"

The girls nodded and leaned toward each other over the table as Casimiro snapped a photo with his phone. "Excellent..." he said slowly as he typed a description and uploaded the photo. "Thank you!" A smile on his face, he left to serve other customers.

Sophie's face turned serious. "Listen," and she leaned forward at the table. "I know I'm still in grade school. But if anything's ever bothering you, you can talk to me, you know. Our family's weird, but I'm pretty okay."

Juliana's face broke out into a huge smile. "I hope you know the same is true about me."

Sophie nodded in acceptance. "So," she continued, "family rumour has it you've joined a dance club at school now? What's that all about?"

Juliana had had her first practice earlier in the week. The energy in her body pumped up as she excitedly told Sophie about it all: the old music, the community hours, and the chance to dance more. She couldn't wait for her first show.

CHAPTER NINETEEN

It was nighttime, and Elisabeth found herself sitting in the back room, a thick, crocheted blanket over her shoulders, and several lanterns—her only source of light in the otherwise dark house—around her sketchbook on the dining room table. As she continued to draw her picture of her confirmation dinner with Konrad-Bátschi, Margarethe-Néni, Georg, and Eva on one side of the table, and Mammi, Samuel, and Deaf Lissi on the other, the events of the day just past flew through her head.

Mammi had indeed lost the baby, but by the time Margarethe-Néni had come to bring the Schuhmacher children home, the house and workshop had been scrubbed clean and Mammi's laundered dress was hanging over the backend of the oven in the front room to dry. Now

Mammi lay sound asleep in her bed and Elisabeth's siblings were also sleeping at last.

"It's almost as though there never was a baby," Elisabeth said to Jesus. "Why did You take it away?" She shaded in Mammi's black headscarf. "How are we supposed to celebrate Your resurrection tomorrow when we have a death to mourn?"

What made this all the more difficult was that there would be no mourning, no funeral. Elisabeth would be expected to continue tomorrow as though nothing had happened. She couldn't even tell her siblings about this.

Elisabeth smudged the black on Mammi's headscarf to soften it a little and then moved over to Georg, colouring in his shirt with a light grey to reflect the cream-coloured linen fabric it was made of.

"He speaks much more to me now," she said to Jesus of Georg. "Anna has taken to him, too, and I believe Rosina isn't far behind." She let out a quiet laugh as she remembered the time out on the *salasch*, when Elisabeth had asked Georg to go into his brother's house and fetch her youngest sister, because Rosina likely wouldn't listen to her. Rosina had indeed listened to Georg, running out, screaming for help in her fear of him while Georg calmly followed. That time was now past.

"Then there was Luki," she said. She looked up at Jesus. "Do you remember when he came in from the animal stalls, all covered in straw? I asked him to clean himself off and he refused. Georg told him to listen to me, and Luki ran back outside."

Now she chuckled. It was funny seeing Georg's serious self in contrast to her siblings' occasional silliness.

"Now I understand why he likes Stefan so much: Stefan is that joyful side that Georg often has trouble trying to find."

She adjusted the shading on Georg's face ever so slightly to give it a hint of joy. "But not too much," she said to herself. Sadness and fear still filled his soul.

"Stefan helps keep those feelings away."

As she continued perfecting her drawing, she mulled over what first Maria and later Mammi had suggested about Stefan: that his missing an arm made him less of a man.

Elisabeth now drew hints of the embroidery that so beautifully adorned the table runner that had lain across the dinner table.

"Would a nice man with two hands really befriend Georg?" she asked herself. "That takes someone who has lived among soldiers to understand. Having two hands doesn't give someone a bigger heart, but helping many men with broken bodies and souls does."

She now shaded in the empty chair at the head of the table.

"I can't keep my family together by myself," she said as she drew, "although I now know I have people who can help me." But after she finished the drawing, she looked at the empty chair, dreading the next day, Easter without Tata.

She closed the book, returned it and her drawing pencils to their drawer in the back room, and turned down the wick of each lantern, extinguishing the flames.

"Good night, Tata," she said as she crept to her bed in the front room.

THAT NIGHT, THE HOUSE QUIET, JULIANA SAT ALONE IN HER bedroom, already in her pyjamas and lying on her bed, propped up by two pillows. Her lamp lit up her room, and she held Omama's book open on her lap to the drawing of the table with several members of her family on either side and the chair at the head of the table empty.

"Opa said that chair was for me, but I think it was really for Mom," she said to herself.

Juliana and Mom had spoken after supper tonight, and although Mom didn't explain much more than what they'd discussed on Thursday, she did apologize and promise to try better.

"I guess I can try, too," she said aloud as though she was talking with Omama. "I mean, your dad was *away*, like, away-away for a long time. Mine comes back after at most eight or nine days."

She longed to touch the drawing, but Opa had told her months ago that she'd smudge the sketches if she did.

"I can at least touch the edge of a page, right, Omama?" she asked. Believing the answer would have been yes, she slid her finger carefully along the edge of the page, tracing it all the way around. It made her feel connected to this girl, her great-grandmother, who had a long time ago touched this page as she drew the pictures.

"Opa said you had a really hard life. I can't imagine what he meant by that." She turned back a page and traced her finger around it, too. "I don't want to make him sad—he's always so happy when he talks about you. But I want to know your story."

She closed the book and held it in both her hands.

"Elisabeth with an *s*," she said. "Somehow, that makes you more alive to me than calling you Omama." She caressed the book's cover. "You drew these when you were my age. That makes you more my friend than my great-grandmother." She tucked the book carefully away in her night table drawer and switched off her light.

"Good night, Elisabeth."

SETTING THE RECORD STRAIGHT

Between Worlds tells a contemporary fictional story together with a story that is historical fiction. In both parts of the book, I've taken facts about life in the time period in which the story is set and included them in a fictional story. In writing novels, the story always comes first (because otherwise this would be a history textbook), so this section explains any important facts that may have been changed to fit the story and adds more background to the story. If you have any questions about what you've read in this or any of the other books in the series, ask away! My contact information is in the "Stay in Touch!" section.

BIRTHDAYS

The previous book, *Between Worlds 5: Hide and Seek*, was all about Mom's birthday, and her family's planning of a large celebration for her in the contemporary storyline. In the historical storyline for this book, you may have wondered why Eva mentions briefly to Elisabeth that Georg's birthday (March 30th) was just around the corner, only to have the story move on without a party.

I set birthdays for each character because the books follow each other in chronological order—they're not episodes that could have happened at any time—and I let readers know when characters turn one year older. That could mean I'd have to write about many birthday parties! However, Germans of this time usually celebrated name days instead of birthdays. For example, everyone named Elisabeth would have celebrated on the same day, instead of everyone who was born on July 27th (Elisabeth's birthday) celebrating their birthday that day.

(Juliana's birthday is June 3rd, in case you're curious.)

HORSEBACK RIDING

As I looked through old photos from Semlak, I realized that no one sat on a horse. Granted, I have only a handful of these photos, and they cannot reflect the full life I'm trying to recreate here. But when I asked members of the older generation of Germans who lived in Romania, Hungary, and Yugoslavia about riding on horses, my suspicions were confirmed: farmers generally drove wagons. If anyone rode atop a horse, though, it was a man: a woman riding a horse was highly improper.

However, it doesn't mean that none of the Germans in Eastern Europe rode horses. In Gara, Hungary, where my paternal grandfather was born, several families bred horses, often to sell to the military. In *Gara*, by Stefan Keiner, there are several photos of men atop horses, but none of women.

BAKING BREAD

Women in Semlak did indeed use troughs carved out from tree trunks to knead bread dough in. According to Rose Mary Keller-Hughes, the Village Coordinator for Semlak at the Donauschwaben Villages Helping Hands website, baking bread typically started the night before, when the baker would take a small amount of sourdough starter (in our parlance) saved from the previous baking day and mix it together with large quantities of flour and water, along with yeast and salt. This large starter dough then rested overnight, before more flour and water were kneaded into it the following morning to create bread dough. You'll find Rose Mary's description of the process here: http://www.dvhh.org/cooking-

donauschwaben-style/yeast-baking/Baking-Bread-
Semlak~keller-hughes.htm.

In this novel, that means Elisabeth would have had to begin baking on a Sunday night, something that would most certainly not have been done. Because adding yeast to sourdough helps with a faster rise, I decided to let Elisabeth begin her bread baking early on a Monday morning so that the story could continue to move forward.

CITY NAMES

Juliana comes across different spellings of Semlak in this book. Because *Between Worlds* is about a German family and its descendants, I chose to retain the German spellings. However, you would not find these spellings on a map. If you'd like to read more online about the locations in Romania, use these spellings:

- Semlak—Semlac
- Temeswar—Timișoara
- Marosch River—Mureș River
- Arad—Arad

STAY IN TOUCH!

If you enjoyed the book, sign up for my monthly newsletter! I write it myself, so it's my words to you. You'll get the following:

- Sneak peeks at upcoming books
- Updates about online and in-person appearances
- Book and writing recommendations
- Recipes I love
- Contests
- And more!

Visit BetweenWorldsYA.com to sign up!

Prefer social media? All my links are listed under my bio, at the end of the book.

ACKNOWLEDGEMENTS

No book comes together on its own. I have a team behind me who helps bring each novel to life. Thank you to historian Daniel Kalman (Hungary) and researcher Levente Csibi (Hungary) for contributing research to the series. I also still use research completed by Crenguta Nicolae and Gabriela Rat, both of Romania. In addition, thank you to Henry Fisher for his feedback on Elisabeth's confirmation, Anne Dreer for her stories about growing up as a German in Eastern Europe, and the Donauschwaben Villages Helping Hands website, volunteers, and contributors. Without their help, I could not have made Semlak come as alive as it has.

More thank-yous go out to my book team: Heather Wright, my writing coach and consulting editor, and Writer #1 of Zwei Writers from K-W; Susan Fish of Storywell, my reviewer and line editor (all remaining errors are mine); Michelle Fairbanks of Fresh Design, my cover designer; and Ariel Hudnall of ZG Communications, my marketing consultant.

Thank you to ali macgee, my mentor, whose guidance with my writing career has been invaluable.

Last, thanks to my family for all their support as I keep writing this series: Mom, Dad, and Kristin as I grew up and still talk to them about this series; and Corey, Khristopher, and Jonnathan who deal with "I'll be down for supper soon!" almost every night.

ABOUT LORI

Photo by Erin Watt Photography

Lori Wolf-Heffner is a former competitive dancer, dance teacher, and theatre manager. She was a member of the first Canadian National Tap Team, back in 1996, under the leadership of Bonnie Dyer, with choreographer Mathew Clark. She's written for *Dance Canada Quarterly*, *just dance!* magazine, and *The Dance Current* (all under Lori Straus).

Fluent in German, Lori lived in Germany for three years, never once realizing just how close she was to some of the villages her ancestors left to migrate to Eastern Europe in the 1700s.

Lori lives in Waterloo, Ontario, Canada, with her husband and two sons. She is a member of The Writers' Union of Canada and the Alliance of Independent Authors.

facebook.com/loriwolfheffner

x.com/LoriWolfHeffner

instagram.com/loriwolfheffner

goodreads.com/lori_wolf-heffner

bookbub.com/author/lori-wolf-heffner

pinterest.com/loriwolfheffner

amazon.com/author/loriwolfheffner

9 781989 465127